The Detective Is Already Dead

7

La detective
es la muerta

nigozyu

Illustration by **Umibouzu**

"It's kind of late for this, but I'm embarrassed that I took that piggyback offer now..."

Nagisa mumbled, then went to stand beside her.

"Mm-hmm. I knew it. Even if we had to push it a bit, this was worth the climb."

Tucking her hair behind her ear, Siesta smiled at the view.

"I have no idea what you're talking about. I was just testing you, to see whether you'd lost your edge."

Charlotte
Arisaka
Anderson

Yui Saikawa

"I hadn't seen you in a long time, Kimizuka, so I was trying to think of the very best outfit for the occasion, and this is what I came up with. How does it look?"

Siesta

Nagisa
Natsunagi

Reloaded

Mia WhitloCk

 **《Calendar》**

11, April	Origin unclear; he lived in a series of different care homes
May	Danny Bryant takes him in
13, April	Lives in an apartment while helping with "handyman" jobs
May	Danny dies
14, April	Lives a routine middle-school life
May	Meets Gekka Shirogane, searches for the truth behind Danny's death
June	Meets Siesta, fights the pseudohuman Bat at ten thousand meters
17, May	Wanders around the world with Siesta, spends his days fighting SPES, encounters Hel, and meets Alicia (Nagisa Natsunagi)
June	Siesta dies
18, May	Lives a routine high-school life
June	Meets Nagisa Natsunagi, investigates her heart's secret Meets Yui Saikawa, fights SPES again
July	Reunites with Charlotte, fights the pseudohuman Chameleon Learns the truth behind Siesta's death, Nagisa Natsunagi's past, and the existence of the Tuners
August	Encounters Scarlet, faces off against and reconciles with Fuubi Kase Meets Mia Whitlock, Bat dies Natsunagi returns her heart to Siesta, and the living and the dead switch places Defeats the leader of SPES, the primordial seed, with help from Hel and the others
September	Natsunagi awakens, Siesta falls asleep
19, December	The Great Cataclysm

The Detective Is Already Dead

7

nigozyu

Illustration by Umibouzu

New York

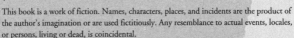

The Detective Is Already Dead, Vol. 7
nigozyu

Translation by Taylor Engel
Cover art by Umibouzu

TANTEI HA MO SHINDEIRU, Vol.7
©nigozyu 2022
First published in Japan in 2022 by KADOKAWA CORPORATION, Tokyo.
English translation rights arranged with KADOKAWA CORPORATION, Tokyo,
through TUTTLE-MORI AGENCY, INC., Tokyo.

Yen On
150 West 30th Street, 19th Floor
New York, NY 10001

Visit us at yenpress.com
facebook.com/yenpress
twitter.com/yenpress
yenpress.tumblr.com
instagram.com/yenpress

First Yen On Edition: March 2024
Edited by Yen On Editorial: Anna Powers
Designed by Yen Press Design: Jane Sohn

Yen On is an imprint of Yen Press, LLC.
The Yen On name and logo are trademarks of Yen Press, LLC.

Library of Congress Cataloging-in-Publication Data
Names: nigozyu, author. | Umibouzu, illustrator. | Engel, Taylor, translator.
Title: The detective is already dead / nigozyu ; illustration by Umibouzu ;
    translation by Taylor Engel.
Other titles: Tantei wa Mou, Shindeiru. English
Description: First Yen On edition. | New York, NY : Yen On, 2021.
Identifiers: LCCN 2021012132 | ISBN 9781975325756 (v. 1 ; trade paperback);
    ISBN 9781975325770 (v. 2 ; trade paperback); ISBN 9781975325794
    (v. 3 ; trade paperback); ISBN 9781975348250 (v. 4 ; trade paperback);
    ISBN 9781975360122 (v. 5 ; trade paperback); ISBN 9781975368975
    (v. 6 ; trade paperback); ISBN 9781975379568 (v. 7 ; trade paperback)
Subjects: GSAFD: Mystery fiction.
Classification: LCC PL873.5.I46 T3613 2021 | DDC 895.63/6—dc23
LC record available at https://lccn.loc.gov/2021012132

ISBNs: 978-1-9753-7956-8 (paperback)
          978-1-9753-7957-5 (ebook)

10 9 8 7 6 5 4 3 2 1

LSC-C

Printed in the United States of America

The Detective Is Already Dead

7

Contents

Prologue

"Is there a detective on the plane?"

That question had made me doubt my ears at first, but it had once launched me into a dazzling adventure.

It wasn't a line you generally heard on passenger planes ten thousand meters in the air.

In a situation like that, people would usually be asking for a doctor or a nurse.

Who'd have believed they'd want a detective? I'd been born with a knack for getting dragged into stuff, so at the time, I'd wondered if it was my fault.

"It's not fair."

In my seat on the plane, I'd heaved one of my usual sighs.

However, that was when things had really started getting unusual.

"Yes, I'm a detective."

The girl who'd spoken had been sitting in the seat on my right.

She had blue eyes and a pale silver bob. Her dress seemed to be modeled on a military uniform, and it flared as she brandished her musket. Once she was on the scene, the incident was over.

The consummately beautiful ace detective.

Her code name was Siesta.

What she wanted was to fulfill her clients' requests and act in their best interests.

For some reason, Siesta appointed me as her assistant. Together, we left on a three-year journey to defeat the enemies of the world—and then death parted us.

At the time, we were fighting an organization called SPES. A member of the enemy's upper ranks, a girl named Hel, defeated Siesta and took her heart.

And so my adventure was over... Or so I thought.

"You're the ace detective?"

A year later, a certain client came to me.

She had red eyes and long, glossy black hair. This high school girl, whose trademark was her red ribbon, pulled me from my tepid routine with her blazing passion.

She was both a client and a proxy detective—her name was Nagisa Natsunagi.

She wanted me to locate someone who'd saved her life.

She pulled me back into the extraordinary, and soon I found myself with a wish: Someday, I'd take Siesta back.

However, resurrecting the dead carried a heavy price. Natsunagi literally risked her life to let Siesta retake her heart.

In the process, she also defeated Seed, our final enemy. This time, we'd won our happy ending.

...Or so it seemed. We'd made just one miscalculation: the "seed" in Siesta's heart.

As long as that was there, someday she'd lose control and become a monster. The only way to treat it was for Siesta to stay asleep and prevent the seed from growing.

When Siesta gave up on everything and tried to get rid of herself, I stood in her way. In the end, with the help of our other friends, I got her to take a long nap instead.

On that day, the ace detective became a sleeping beauty, surrounded by the blissful scent of black tea.

That ended the first phase of our adventure.

However, it really was too soon for an epilogue.

* * *

So that I'd be able to wake Siesta up one day, I left on a journey with companions who were hoping for the same thing.

"I'll always be your right arm, Kimihiko, and I'll be your left eye as well."

"I'm your enemy, Kimizuka. When you take a wrong step, I'll slap you."

"It's okay, Kimizuka. Your wish and all of ours will come true."

"Yeah. Let's go on a journey to save our friend."

Then, after living out a dazzling adventure that lasted more than a year, we got through the mother of all disasters, which would later come to be known as "the Great Cataclysm"—

—and at last, we worked a miracle.

It's been a year since then, and seven years since it all began.

I—Kimihiko Kimizuka—am twenty now, a legal adult. I'm soaking from the top of my head to the tips of my toes in "the sequel," an ordinary life.

Am I okay with that, you ask?

Sure. It's not like I'm causing trouble for anybody.

I mean, it's true, isn't it?

The detective is already—

Chapter 1

◆ The mystery starts with a love scene

"Look, look! The bath's glowing!"

A girl's voice echoed from the bathroom.

Considering what sort of hotel this was, it wasn't odd for the bath to shimmer like an aurora or to spout bubbles.

"Come on, aren't you going to come look?"

I was sitting on the double bed by myself in silence when she prompted me again.

Yeesh. What is she trying to lure me into doing? "We didn't come here to play, Nagisa," I told the girl. Actually, she was old enough now that I should call her a woman.

She poked her head out of the bathroom, then came over to me. For some reason, she was smiling faintly. "If we're not playing, does that mean we're serious?"

The room was illuminated by indirect light.

Sitting down on the bed next to me, she looked up at me with a mischievous smile. "I mean, we're spending one of the first nights of a new year in a place like this... You know?"

Makeup suited her even better now than it had in high school. Her already well-defined features were even more attractive, and as I sat there with nothing to do, her rouged lips whispered sweetly to me.

We were more grown-up than we'd been when we met.

Of course we were. It had been more than two years since she'd hauled me up by my shirtfront in that classroom after school. Both Nagisa and I were well past the legal age. We weren't kids anymore.

"I know. Want me to put my fingers in your mouth?" Gently, Nagisa pushed me down onto the bed. "You liked that, didn't you, Kimihiko?"

When had we started calling each other by our first names? We'd said and done so much together that I couldn't remember those little details.

"That's a fetish of yours, isn't it—letting a girl slobber all over you."

"That rumor isn't just exaggerated; it was made up entirely."

What started it was your shoving your fingers down my throat in that classroom after school.

"But they even call it the stabber finger."

"Are you trying to run me through or something? It's called the pointer finger. Because you use it to point at people." This was how our conversations usually went, and I gave a little sigh.

"Your eyelashes sure are long."

Nagisa's face suddenly got a lot closer. Her perfume was that familiar citrus scent. I thought its calming fragrance expressed Nagisa's (surprisingly delicate) feelings really well.

"Kimihiko."

She was right in front of me now. Her figure had also matured quite a bit.

"Nagisa."

Our lips drew closer and closer. Nagisa shut her eyes. And then—

"Except we're here for work."

My eyes snapped open. I flung Nagisa onto the bed, then focused my ears on *the sounds from the next room over which were coming through my Bluetooth headset.*

"...I mean, I knew that. I also figured this was where things were going and rolled with it, okay? Geez, who just throws girls onto beds like that, huh?"

Nagisa was muttering something, but more importantly... "We've got a winner here. Definitely guilty."

I handed the headset to Nagisa, who took it grudgingly. The audio from the next room over was...

"Ohh, this is... Yes. Absolutely." Awkwardly, Nagisa averted her eyes. Considering what type of hotel this was, I doubt I need to tell you what was happening over there.

"Huh? Oh, they're really branching out. Hm, they're putting that in there? Whoa…"

"We didn't come here to find out what modern bugs are capable of, but we sure did anyway."

We'd planted the bug in our target's bag ahead of time. Now that we'd gotten this audio, we had solid proof.

"I feel bad for the guy who hired us, but we'd better let him know about this."

I took out my smartphone and started putting together a report on our infidelity investigation.

We'd gotten this request at the end of last year from an office drone who suspected his wife was cheating on him. The client's wife was a model at the top of her field, and they'd gotten married a few months ago in a top secret ceremony. However…

"His gorgeous model wife is cheating on him with a guy in her industry. That's rough." Nagisa sighed uncomfortably.

"Yeah, and the client is… Maybe it's rude to say this, but he's a bland office worker. If a male model steals his wife, the news might hit him extra hard."

"Yeah, the guy she's cheating with is superhot."

"Yeah. By the way, Nagisa, you can take the headset off now."

"…Wh-what are you talking about?"

It seemed mean to interrupt when she was enjoying herself so much, but I took the headset back, then immediately texted the report to our client.

"Still, how do you suppose an ordinary office worker managed to convince a model to marry him?"

I'd been curious about that myself. Not only that, but here she was, cheating on him just a few months after their wedding. It was all pretty weird.

"Well, anyway, we've got this one solved now, don't we? Even if it's left a bad taste in our mouths," Nagisa said, tucking her hair behind her ear.

"Yeah. Want to stand by until the target leaves the room?" Figuring that would be about two hours from now, I checked my watch. We'd probably be home by dinnertime.

"I see. What will we do while we're waiting?" Nagisa asked. She was sitting with her legs kicked out to the sides in an M shape, and she looked up

at me through her lashes. The turtleneck she was wearing showed off her curves; she really had matured since high school, in several ways.

"I know you're not actually that dense, Kimihiko."

The heater was on in here; the room was a little warm, and Nagisa's cheeks were flushed.

"...Well, I guess there are some things you have to face head-on."

I needed a way to productively kill two whole hours, so I rummaged in my bag for a certain item. "I'm not done with any of my winter term homework. Help me out."

I was lucky to have a brilliant friend in the same seminar. At this rate, I was perilously close to getting held back a year. Rolling my shoulders, I opened my laptop.

"I wish you'd get held back a year for your whole life."

That sulky face of Nagisa's was the only thing adulthood hadn't changed.

About two hours later, as predicted, there was motion from the room next door.

"Great. Nagisa, let's go."

"How about a thank-you?"

I saved the report, which I'd finished with Nagisa's help, then we grabbed our stuff and went after the target. Once we'd seen the pair enter the elevator, we ran down the stairs. Fortunately, it wasn't too many floors.

"There they are. That pair in coats."

Outside the hotel, in a gloomy alley with the sun almost below the horizon, Nagisa pointed at a couple in overcoats. They had their arms linked companionably. They probably had no idea their rendezvous had been witnessed.

"What do you want to do? Should we keep following them?" I asked Nagisa.

We already had proof of the affair. There didn't seem to be much point in shadowing the couple any longer... But just as I was mulling over our options, it happened.

About fifty meters ahead of us, the woman we were following gave a short scream.

What had happened? What was going to happen?

As we started running to catch up, we saw that a man had dashed out of an alley. He had a blade in his hand, and he was shouting. "Traitor!"

"—! Is that our client?"

In the distance, the woman's lover held her close, protecting her. For a moment, the man with the knife hesitated, but then he screamed again and raised his weapon above his head.

Nagisa and I wouldn't make it in time. The man's blade began to descend toward the other man's back.

"Argh, not again."

I sighed at my own incompetence, or maybe because *she'd* stolen yet another march on me. Next to me, Nagisa was probably feeling the same way. We stopped, weary but relieved, and exchanged looks.

Did we have time for that, you ask?

Sure. The incident was already over.

"Nice try, but no. Put down the knife and surrender."

A figure in white had appeared out of nowhere and pinned the man with the knife.

The ace detective had probably been ready well in advance, then carelessly fallen asleep. But once again, she'd waltzed in to steal the best part.

"Assistant, don't just stand there. Hurry up and call the police."

Her elegant dress hadn't changed a bit, but she did look a little more grown-up than she had when we first met.

She was the keenly intelligent, talented, beautiful, flawless, and unimpeachable ace detective.

The only reply I could offer her was one of my typical sarcastic ones:

"Couldn't you have helped us out a little sooner, Siesta?"

◆ Detective, assistant, and chief

The detective agency was on the second floor of a mixed-use building.

"So, how did you make it work this time?" I asked Siesta. I was leaning back into a well-worn sofa, opening the box of pizza that had just been delivered.

After the uproar near the hotel, the man with the knife had been safely handed over to the police. By the time we'd finally made it back here, it was well after sunset, and I still didn't have a complete picture of the incident.

"Oh, I want a slice with lots of shrimp."

Siesta had been in her usual spot at the back of the office, typing on her computer. Now she was drifting over to the freshly baked pizza, like a butterfly drawn to a flower.

"Siesta, are you listening to me?"

"I'm always listening to the voice of your heart. Snarf-snarf."

"If you're gonna eat with sound effects, at least be cute about it, wouldja?" I shot back, and I meant it. Siesta had taken a seat across from me and was stuffing her face.

"Once he knew for sure that she was cheating, the client flew into a rage and attacked his wife and her lover... Isn't that what happened?" Nagisa asked. Bringing over three glasses of soda, she set them on the table in front of us.

"Well, one of our original assumptions was wrong." Now that she'd finished a slice of pizza, Siesta finally began answering our questions. "The man with the knife—our client—wasn't married to that model."

Nagisa and I exchanged looks. Neither of us had been expecting that one.

"The client was *stalking* her. When he suspected she had a real partner, he hired a detective to find out for sure."

...I see. In that case, we'd basically aided and abetted a stalker.

"But what about the copy of the family register he brought as proof that they were married?"

"Probably a forgery. There are people who'll take on under-the-table projects like that."

"So you realized he was lying back then, Siesta?"

"I didn't find anything suspicious in the documents right away, but what he told us about his wife seemed rather unnatural."

"How so?" Nagisa asked, sitting down beside her.

"It was almost as if he'd memorized an online profile. Superficially, he knew a lot about his wife, but there was no substance to it." Siesta took a long swig of soda, then added, "For example, I know the things my assistant commonly says in his sleep, and that he likes his fried eggs with soy sauce, and I've seen him scrunch up his face when he takes powdered medicines. I know everything about him."

"Huh? Are you trying to one-up me?"

"That's the sort of information you can't know if you've never lived with your partner. The client didn't have any of that."

Oh. So the client—or rather, the criminal—must've felt as if he knew the woman just from looking at her data. He'd probably started to think he was the only one who could understand her or something.

"I see," said Nagisa. "You know, it did feel vaguely off to me, too."

Now that she knew what had really been going on, Nagisa nodded as if everything made sense to her.

She was right: Even in the hotel, she'd seemed to think there was something odd about the incident.

"Hrmm. I've got to try harder. I'm already studying for school anyway," Nagisa told herself, smacking her cheeks sharply.

Like me, Nagisa was majoring in psychology. According to her, there was a motive behind every incident, and behind that motive was a human heart. In order to grow as a detective, she said she needed to better understand the mind.

"So I was the only one who didn't notice anything, then?"

Geez. If Siesta had figured it out, she could have filled me in.

"They say if you want to fool your enemies, first fool your friends, right?"

"That's not fair... Well, I'd like to say it's not, but were you trying to accomplish something by doing that?"

"If we were all on the same page, we wouldn't be able to handle unforeseen situations. It's like the way the pilot and copilot eat different meals on a flight to avoid any possibility of food poisoning. It's risk management—we should be coming at this from different angles."

"You mean even if we all have the same basic goal, sometimes it's effective to intentionally have individual perspectives and do different things?"

I didn't even have to think very hard to see we'd always worked that way.

"Actually, I found this a little while ago. It's a private account." Siesta held up her phone, displaying someone's social media page.

"Does this belong to that model?" Nagisa asked. In a post, the OP mentioned feeling like they were being followed. The woman must have noticed her stalker.

"But it's an anonymous account. How did you find it?"

"I just applied the same method I used to identify your account way back when."

"You tracked down my account?"

And apparently she wasn't planning on telling me how. This sucks.

"...Well, I'll turn a blind eye to the past for now. Point is, you thought the woman might have a stalker, so you were on the scene again today."

"Yes, although it was only a theory. I hadn't completely ruled out the possibility that the client might have married the model in secret."

However, because Siesta had noticed all the possibilities, we'd avoided a worst-case scenario.

"I used to be able to resolve these things a bit more neatly." She smiled faintly, remembering distant days.

When she'd been a Tuner, Siesta had had *a certain special notebook* that granted its bearer every sort of qualification there was. If she'd used that, it would have been easy for her to check with the ward office and find out if the client and model really were married.

However, at this point, she didn't have that sort of authority.

"I'm just a detective now."

Right; she wasn't a Tuner or the Ace Detective anymore.

She was only a detective, and...

"You're also the chief here, remember?" I told her.

Siesta smiled. "Oh, that's right."

She was the chief, Nagisa was the detective, and I was their assistant.

About a year ago, peace had abruptly come to the world. The string of global crises that would later be known as "the Great Cataclysm" were resolved by the Ace Detective and many other heroes, and the world was saved.

As proof that perpetual peace had arrived, the Oracle, Mia Whitlock, had lost her ability to see the future. That meant global crises were no longer being recorded in the sacred text.

It had been a year since the Tuner system itself had been dissolved. Siesta had established this detective agency because she believed that, even in this peaceful world, somebody somewhere would still need justice. Nagisa and I had agreed, and we'd kept on working with her even as university students.

"Well, I'm not very fond of the name you gave us, Kimi."

For no apparent reason, Siesta started criticizing the agency's name, even though we'd settled on it a whole year back. Sheesh. As always, she'd had me choose because she couldn't be bothered, and now all she did was complain about it.

"Hey, it's a good name. The Shirogane Detective Agency."

I'd borrowed the name of a certain benefactor of mine. I didn't know why, but Siesta wasn't happy about that.

"Still, the year just started, and I'm already wiped out." I stretched, then relaxed.

This request had come in at the end of the year, and it had taken us until today, January 2, to solve it. I'd known there wouldn't be holidays at any detective agency run by Siesta, but still.

"Should we relax and make our first shrine visit of the year tomorrow?" Siesta suggested unexpectedly.

Come to think of it, she'd always been the type to put seasonal events right up there with work.

"Hooray! A chance to wear a kimono!" Nagisa agreed enthusiastically, flexing her muscles.

It might be a break, but going anywhere with Siesta and Nagisa was bound to become a headache in one way or another. I felt I should replenish my energy stores while I could, which was why I bit into a slice of pizza. Just then…

"It looks like we have a job," Siesta said. When I turned to look, she was opening the window. Cold night air blew in, and I put up the collar of my jacket. Then, with a rustle of wings, something flew into the agency.

"Thank you. I'll take this," Siesta told it, relieving our visitor (an owl) of the letter it held in its beak.

"What are you, some kind of wizard?"

"Don't you know about carrier pigeons, Kimi? They can fly a thousand kilometers."

My comment had been specifically because our visitor was an owl, not a pigeon, but more importantly... "Who's the job request from?" I couldn't tell from her expression.

Nagisa watched her, too, waiting for an answer.

Siesta's eyes remained on the letter for a little while longer. Then, finally, she looked up.

"For the first time in a year, we have a summons from the Federation Government."

◆ Proxy Ace Detectives

Thanks to the Federation Government's orders, the next evening found us in the city of a thousand temples—Kyoto. We'd spent a little over two hours on the bullet train, and no sooner had we reached our station than a shiny black car had legally abducted us.

"I wanted to have some dango or yatsuhashi first," Nagisa grumbled. She was kicking her feet like a kid, protesting the way we were being treated.

"Yeah. I was just wishing they'd brought us over in first class," I said, adding a gripe of my own.

That said, these were demands for our employer.

"We won't necessarily be able to write it off as a work expense, so no." Gazing out the window, Siesta spoke like a business owner. "After all, we don't know whether they're going to be our client yet."

By "they," she meant the Federation Government—the entity who'd sent the carrier owl.

The letter hadn't mentioned any specifics. They'd just told the three of us to come to this location, at this time, on this date.

"Man. Not fair." The words were out of my mouth before I'd even thought about them.

I hadn't been saying that phrase much lately. However, right now, those were the only appropriate words for the situation I—well, technically, the two girls—had been placed in.

What business could the Federation Government have with the former Ace Detectives, after all this time?

We spent another forty minutes in the car before reaching our destination.

Just as the sun was setting, we followed our driver-turned-guide up a gravel path. Before long, an enormous Buddhist temple came into view.

"Isn't this an important cultural asset?" Nagisa murmured. The building looked like something that would show up in a Japanese history reference book. I was pretty sure it was off-limits to the general public, but our guide gestured straight at the entrance, telling us to go in. Then I realized that all the pigeons on the temple grounds had turned to look at us.

We took off our shoes and stepped into the main temple, where an expanse of hard wooden flooring lay before us. Off to the sides, several dozen masked servants dressed in white stood in long rows.

"...Why do they all have spears?" That seemed ominous. I swallowed hard.

"Assistant, look." Siesta pointed at the back of the room.

There was a dimly lit Buddha hall back there. The hall enshrined a huge Buddha, and someone was sitting in front of it. They wore the same mask as the servants, but their clothing resembled a court lady's twelve-layered kimono. Between that and the long hair, it seemed safe to say that this was a woman.

"A Federation Government dignitary, hm?"

She was in a completely different class from the servants who were waiting off to the sides. Even though we'd grumbled on the way here, we now straightened up, whether we felt like it or not. We seated ourselves in a row, kneeling formally, with Nagisa in the middle.

"I apologize for summoning you so abruptly."

For a moment, I didn't know who had spoken. Then I realized that the dignitary was bowing so low that her forehead touched the floor. She was apologizing to us?

"Nagisa, do you know that official?" I asked. Nagisa was kneeling formally beside me. This much humility coming from a representative of the

Federation Government was extremely weird. All the dignitaries I'd ever dealt with had been much more overbearing, mechanical, and sort of lacking in humanity.

"No, I don't know her. I doubt Siesta does, either."

On Nagisa's other side, Siesta gazed at the dignitary dubiously, but she was the first to speak. "And? What did you want with us?"

"First, take a look at this."

The masked dignitary raised her head.

In the next instant, a vivid image was projected onto the Buddha hall behind her. It was something like projection mapping that used the uneven background as a screen.

However, what it showed made me want to cover my eyes.

"The corpses of government officials?" I heard myself say. And I hadn't meant "corpse," singular. The beheaded bodies of several masked dignitaries were projected on every surface of the Buddha hall as 3D images, one after another.

"At present, Federation Government high officials are being assassinated all over the world."

...The Federation Government ruled the world from the shadows, and the murderer was only targeting them? If that was really happening, that would be...

"So it's a new global crisis?" Siesta asked, speaking for all of us.

"Wait, though. Aren't global crises a whole lot rarer these days?" Nagisa broke in. As she said, no new enemies of the world had appeared on Earth in the past year. As if to corroborate this, Mia's clairvoyance hadn't activated even once. In that light, what sort of crisis could the killing of these dignitaries be?

"We view them as an 'unknown crisis,' which even the Oracle couldn't detect."

That was the name the masked dignitary across from us gave the situation.

"We see the basic problem. Why did you summon Siesta and Nagisa for this, though?" I asked, even though I already knew the answer.

"I'll speak plainly: We would like the two former Ace Detectives to investigate."

Ridiculous. Though this had nothing to do with me, I still almost said that out loud.

And my emotions were justified. Their mission as Ace Detectives was over. Why should the Federation Government get to rope them into something now?

"Take a close look at this," the official said, and the image zoomed in on a certain spot to reveal—

"*Those are tentacle fragments.* Not from just any tentacle, either. They're fragments of the weapons wielded by the pseudohumans you once fought. We believe someone is misusing their power to kill these dignitaries."

…She was right. More than two years ago now, our group had fought Seed's pseudohumans. But that battle was over, and so were the sacrifices made to end it.

"Are you saying we haven't finished cleaning up yet?" Nagisa asked. Was the mission still ongoing?

"No. But given these facts, it is true that when we found these things at the scenes of the incidents, we wished to have the Ace Detective's help once more. In other words, Miss Natsunagi and Miss Siesta, in accordance with a special measure outlined in the Federal Charter, we would like to temporarily appoint you as proxy Ace Detectives."

Nagisa and Siesta exchanged looks. Both the reason for this summons and the substance of the request were completely unexpected. Then, for some reason, the two of them turned to me.

"Why do you look more irritated about this than anybody else, Kimihiko?" Nagisa asked.

"…I didn't know I did," I said.

Siesta showed me her hand mirror. "See?"

Oh yeah. My eyes looked about twenty percent meaner than usual. How did that happen? …No, I actually knew the answer to that, too. I was just pretending not to.

Even so, for now… "It's not my decision anyway. What we do is up to you two."

Siesta and Nagisa nodded, then turned back the official.

"All right. I'll take this Ace Detective job for you.".

"Mm, so will I. Just temporarily, though."

Right. They wouldn't leave a job half done. I'd known this was how it would go.

"We appreciate your help. Take these." The woman took two notebooks out of her robes. I hadn't seen those things in a while. Having them would make Siesta and Nagisa Tuners again.

"I'll get them."

When the other two started to stand up, I stopped them and got to my feet instead.

I respected their choice—I couldn't reject their work or how they felt. Even so, one thing just didn't sit right with me.

"Detectives always put their lives on the line in a fight. Show us you're serious about this, too."

Don't you run. Don't just give them orders without even showing your face. I won't allow it. Walking up to the official, I reached for her mask.

The masked servants who stood on either side of us all pointed their spears at me.

"It's fine." The official stopped them with two words. "I apologize for my rudeness."

She removed her mask.

"From now on, then, I will wear my true face with you. There is just a little more that I must tell you."

Long gray hair spilled over her shoulders, and moss-green eyes gazed straight up at me. I couldn't see any emotion in her expression, but it was full of dignity.

She was a lovely girl whose face still held hints of childish softness.

◆ The name of the messenger who announces peace is...

"I deeply apologize for my repeated rudeness."

Now unmasked, the young dignitary bowed her head.

We'd relocated to what appeared to be a tatami-floored tea room next to the main hall.

"It's quite late for this, but please do enjoy."

The girl offered me tea and sweets—dango and yatsuhashi. Had someone told her about the conversation we'd had in the car? But the one who'd wanted to eat these had been Nagisa...

"I'm terribly sorry. Miss Nagisa and Miss Siesta have various steps to complete..."

She and I were the only ones here. Nagisa and Siesta were in another room, going through the procedures for gaining temporary authority as Tuners. Since there was nothing I could do about that, I took another bite of dango and studied the young dignitary.

Although she'd removed her mask, she was still dressed in those kimono-like robes. Between her clothes and the quiet, tidy way she sat, she reminded me of a *hina* doll. Her features seemed more European than anything, though, and although she was still young, she was truly beautiful. This was the first time I'd ever seen a Federation Government dignitary's real face. It made me conscious of the fact that there really had been living, breathing humans beneath those masks.

"...The kimono as well?" Although the girl had remained expressionless all this time, her eyes now wavered slightly. "Shall I remove the kimono, as well as the mask?"

Apparently she'd misinterpreted my attention. What an imagination she had.

"You did say I should show my sincerity," she went on.

"If that was what I'd meant, I'd be a failure of a human being," I replied.

"My apologies. That was a dignitary joke."

"I've never even heard of such a thing." How had she managed to say that with a straight face?

"It's a method of communication. In our advance investigations, we learned that you are very fond of playing around with women, Mr. Kimihiko."

"Who told you that? At least call it something besides 'playing around.'"

Geez. Her face was cool, but this was what she was really like? She didn't seem like she was trying to do a bit with me. She was serious, humble, and capable of being considerate, but she marched to the beat of her own drum: These were my impressions of this girl.

"What's your name?"

She'd somehow managed to take the wind out of my sails. Without really meaning to, I asked her for her name.

"Noel de Lupwise," she said, looking me straight in the eye. "My code name as a government official is simply 'Lupwise.'"

"If you've managed to become a Federation Government high official at that age, you're really racing up the ladder."

"The Lupwise family is descended from the French aristocracy, and our position in the Federation Government is hereditary."

Noel told me a little more about herself.

She'd become a government official three years ago, when her older brother, who should have been the next head of the family, had vanished. While she hadn't yet gotten many opportunities to handle important jobs, the Federation Government was currently short on people—partly due to the "unknown crisis" she'd just told us about—so even newcomers like her were being put to work.

"I understand the situation, sort of, but...if they're focused on resolving this unknown crisis, and you're new, wasn't there someone who was more suited to the job?"

For example, one of the dignitaries we'd dealt with before had been a crafty old woman code-named Ice Doll. A while back, she'd given the Ace Detective plenty of orders.

"Yes. In fact, other officials are already working on it as well. However, they have another large task to accomplish right now. That was what I wanted to tell you about," Noel said. That was why she'd originally called me to this room; she'd said there was more to discuss.

"It's the Ritual of Sacred Return," she went on, using a phrase I'd never heard before. "Two weeks from now, a peace ceremony celebrating the one-year anniversary of the resolution of the Great Cataclysm will take place, led by the Federation Government. Since the detectives and their assistant saved the world, we would like to have you participate in the ceremony."

Noel held out an invitation.

Apparently, all the former Tuners, any others who'd contributed to the resolution of the Great Cataclysm, and some global VIPs were being invited to this ceremony.

"You're holding it in France?"

"Yes. I know it's very far away, but do you think you could attend?"

It was to be in two weeks. Winter break would be over by then, but it wasn't like we weren't allowed to take time off from university.

"What's going to happen during this ritual, specifically?"

"I believe a similar concept from Japanese culture would be *Otakiage*," Noel answered.

Otakiage. That's the Shinto ritual where they burn old, used-up charms and things.

"During the Ritual of Sacred Return, the sacred texts compiled by the Oracles will be burned in order to purge past crises and pray for new peace."

"...That sounds kind of religious. So you're going to burn all the sacred texts?"

Mia had shown them to me a few years ago, and I was pretty sure there had been more than a hundred thousand of them then. If they meant to burn those in some kind of order, wouldn't it take them longer than three full days?

"No, not all of them. However, we must burn the origin text, no matter what."

"Origin text"? I'd never heard of that.

"It is also referred to as the original sacred text. Possessing it serves as proof that one is the legitimate Oracle. It's written in a language only Oracles can read, and it's said to hold rules regarding the sacred texts...but even I don't know if that's true."

Even ordinary members of the Federation Government weren't allowed to read the sacred texts, and apparently the origin text was even more restricted.

"I'm told that the origin text has a certain special power. By burning it, the Oracle's God-given abilities will be formally returned, which will serve as proof that no further crises will occur on Earth," Noel said. "...Although I've only heard that from others. The Oracle knows the details."

"Then, once the Ritual of Sacred Return is over, Mia and the other Tuners will be officially discharged?"

"In the final analysis, yes, that is what it would mean. At the very least, the Federation Government will no longer ask the former Tuners to resolve crises…I'm aware that the request I've just made seems to contradict this, and I do apologize for that."

So the Federation Government planned to hold the Ritual of Sacred Return in order to set the Tuners free, but the "unknown crisis" of these dignitary killings had broken out right before it was to happen. The timing was incredibly bad, and Siesta and Nagisa had ended up getting the short end of the stick.

"All right, I understand. I'll fill the other two in later."

The two detectives were the main invitees to the ritual. I was only their assistant, and I should respect their decision.

Even so…

"Noel, would you promise me something?" I bowed my head to the official from the world's government. "If Siesta and Nagisa solve this case, and the Ritual of Sacred Return ends without incident, I want you to release them from their mission as Tuners entirely this time."

I gazed at the tatami flooring, then closed my eyes.

"Yes, I promise," she answered promptly. I opened my eyes again. "But why would you go that far, Mr. Kimihiko?"

That was simple. I raised my head. "My wish is—"

◆ A thousand worlds, one wish

"Hurry up or I'll leave you behind, Assistant."

We were on a mountain path, long after sundown. Siesta was climbing the stone stairs ahead of me, but she turned halfway back to glance at me.

The meeting with Noel de Lupwise had ended about two hours earlier. I'd met back up with the detectives, and now, for some reason, I was sweating my way through a nighttime hike. I hadn't gotten much exercise lately, and it was hitting my legs and lower back pretty hard.

"Why are we doing this, anyway?"

"Well, we promised we'd make our first shrine visit of the year today, didn't we?" Siesta said. She was wearing a formal kimono that was mostly white, and there was an ornamental hairpin in her pale silver hair instead of her usual clip.

True, we'd made plans for a shrine visit last night at the detective agency. The Federation Government's abrupt summons had changed those plans, but now we'd returned to our original goal. We'd just passed through the famous thousand torii gates and were heading for the shrine beyond them.

"I wasn't picturing anything this serious, though."

If we were just paying a visit to a shrine, there was a perfectly fine hall of worship much closer to the entrance, but Siesta had said "That would be boring" and started climbing the mountain. In a formal kimono. Ignoring the cold.

"Don't assume I'm a normal woman."

"Yeah, no normal woman would say that."

Siesta smiled and started walking again.

"Still, this place is pretty creepy."

I knew it was sacred ground, but all those torii gates and fox statues made it feel ominous. Granted, it would probably seem a bit different during the day.

"People do say that torii gates might connect to eternity and the afterlife."

I wasn't able to immediately process the two words Siesta had said.

"That's this world and the next world. In other words, the realm of the dead might be just beyond those torii gates."

"Give me a break. Horror's not my thing."

... Besides. I didn't really want to hear Siesta talk about that stuff.

Siesta seemed to have figured that out from my expression; she smiled wryly and apologized. "Maybe it wasn't the realm of the dead. Maybe it was some fantasy parallel universe. There are as many other worlds as there are torii gates."

"That sounds like something from a picture book. Maybe I would've been able to enjoy it when I was a kid."

As we were talking, soft footsteps padded up behind us. "Listen! I keep telling you to wait for me!"

When I turned back, there was Nagisa. She was also wearing a formal kimono and traditional sandals, and her expression was half-angry, half-tearful. I'd been walking pretty slowly, but the distance between us kept widening.

"Geez, it's all red." Having managed to catch up to us, Nagisa sighed, rubbing the place where the thong of her sandal ran between her toes.

Walking was probably going to hurt her. Sighing, I offered Nagisa my back. We wouldn't have to worry about how we looked to others here anyway.

"Huh? You'll carry me?"

"I can manage three minutes max."

"You're a pretty unreliable hero." Laughing, Nagisa climbed onto my back, and I felt the softness and heat of her body. Once she was situated, I started walking slowly.

"………"

Someone was giving us a pointed look.

"What's the matter, Siesta? Aren't you going to go?"

"…Not that it matters or anything."

Siesta's answer didn't quite match my question as she walked on ahead in a huff. Her shoulders slumped a little.

"Siesta's cute like that sometimes." Nagisa smiled next to my ear. I agreed with her just a bit, although I didn't say so out loud.

Taking breaks now and then, we kept passing through those endless torii gates until we finally reached our destination. There was a small shrine and yet another torii gate; the moonlight gave them a mystical feeling. From that open space, we could look out over the city.

"Mm-hmm. I knew it. Even if we had to push it a bit, this was worth the climb." Tucking her hair behind her ear, Siesta smiled at the view.

"It's kind of late for this, but I'm embarrassed that I took that piggyback offer now…" Nagisa mumbled, then went to stand beside her.

An illuminated torii gate and two girls in formal kimonos at the peak of a small mountain, under a starry sky—a scene out of a fantasy.

I hung back slightly to take it in.

…No, it wasn't the scene I was focused on. It was those two. I gazed at the backs of the girls who'd just agreed to be temporary Ace Detectives.

A little while later, Nagisa and Siesta seemed to notice that I was being oddly quiet. They turned around, almost in sync. I shook my head, telling them it was nothing.

"You're both planning to participate in the Ritual of Sacred Return, aren't you?"

I'd told them what I'd heard from Noel on our way up here, but apparently I hadn't needed to. Someone had relayed that information to them while they were going through the procedures for becoming proxy Ace Detectives.

"Yes—there's going to be a ball, isn't there? We'll get to wear evening dresses! I can't wait," Nagisa said.

And then there was Siesta. "I hear there'll be a banquet after the ceremony. Of course I'll go."

"Your reasons for participating have nothing to do with the actual event."

Of course, the main event was the burning of the origin text, but there would also be a ball and a banquet to entertain the guests. Apparently, the ceremony really was meant to celebrate the resolution of the Great Cataclysm as well.

"Before that, though, we'll have to resolve that 'unknown crisis.'"

"Right. In just two weeks, hm...? We're going to be busy."

Siesta drew a quiet, deep breath, and Nagisa stretched emphatically.

Ideally, we'd neutralize the threat before the Ritual of Sacred Return, which was meant to symbolize the achievement of peace. I'd promised Noel we'd contact her at our discretion whenever we made any progress.

But was it going to be possible to get it under control in just two weeks? In all the previous global crises the Ace Detective had tackled, we'd had to fight for several years and make many sacrifices. Besides, the current detective hadn't been involved with the world for quite a while. Would we be able to make up for that in such a short time frame?

"Every building with a light on has someone in it, doesn't it?" Nagisa said, out of nowhere. She was gazing at the city. "In every life, there will always be pain and sadness, and nights when people want to scream that they wish tomorrow wouldn't come, but...I'd like to be the sort of person who can reach out and help them through it. Because once, someone saved me that way," she said, reminiscing.

"Yes, let's do it. We'll save people, towns, big cities, nations, and then—someday, we'll save the world again," Siesta declared, focusing on the distant future.

The air was crystal clear here, at the top of a mountain on a winter night. As the two women looked at the lights of the town, the spotlights that shone on the torii gates dimly illuminated their shapes.

"Oh, I see."

It wasn't like how it had been before.

There were two of them here now.

Two grown, living detectives were here. In that case, I was sure…

After that, we made a late first shrine visit. We tossed coins into the offering box beyond the torii gate, bowing and clapping twice before the altar. Then we put our hands together and prayed to the gods.

Worries and prayers. Wishing "I don't care how you do it, I want you to help me." Way back when, I'd only had one wish: I'd wanted to wake Siesta from her eternal slumber.

In order to make that forbidden wish a reality, we'd left on a dazzling journey. We'd given up many things in exchange, and yet we'd made it through the Great Cataclysm to arrive at a miracle. The sleeping detective had awakened and come home to us.

Now we had these peaceful days, where the world didn't even need the Tuners anymore. We'd won. We'd overcome every sort of global crisis and injustice. So what was I wishing for now? Just one thing.

Let the detectives who saved the world live quietly and happily from now on.

That was the last thing I'd told Noel, and now I silently said it again as a prayer.

◆ The guard dog in the iron cage

"Sorry to keep you waiting."

It was the day after we got back from Kyoto.

As I stood in front of the station, checking my watch, I heard a click and felt a gun muzzle shoved against the back of my neck.

Actually, that was a misunderstanding: When I turned around, I saw that Siesta was merely making a "gun" gesture with her thumb and forefinger. She might have temporarily become the Ace Detective again, but she didn't have her beloved musket back yet.

"That's a new look for you."

We were about to head out on an errand, and instead of her usual dress or the formal kimono she'd worn yesterday, Sierra was in casual clothes: baggy jeans and a patterned jacket. The cap she wore gave her a boyish look—or maybe it was closer to street style. Either way, she didn't seem like her usual self at all, and I ended up looking her over carefully.

"Ogling women like that usually gets you arrested." With a chilly sigh, Siesta returned my gaze.

"Only 'usually'? Does that mean I'm safe this time?"

"As long as I'm the one you're ogling, yes," Siesta retorted, then resettled her cap on her head.

"What happened to your regular clothes?"

"I wanted to wear the outfit I bought when Nagisa and I went shopping."

"You didn't invite me to that party."

"Why are you trying to crash a girls' outing?"

"I'm glad you two get along so well."

Siesta and Nagisa were more than work colleagues—they were best friends.

A tragedy had torn them apart once, but now they'd finally managed to regain the friendship they'd had.

"I do feel a little strange in clothes someone else picked out, though." Even as she spoke, Siesta was gazing at her outfit happily.

She's changed a bit, I thought.

I didn't know exactly which time to compare to, but Siesta was clearly softer around the edges than she had been when I'd first met her, or when we'd traveled together. She'd started smiling.

Of course, her old attitude—indifferent, to the point of stoicism—had probably been her defining trait, but I'd wanted her to be more human, more susceptible to trivial emotions. And so this Siesta was the one I—

"Shall we go?"

As I stood lost in thought, she held out her pale left hand to me.

That hand was the one thing that hadn't changed.

It was the same at ten thousand meters, and also here, with our feet firmly planted on the ground, this close to each other.

After that, Siesta and I climbed into a taxi and went to prison.

By "prison," I mean exactly what it sounds like...but I wasn't an incoming convict. I'd come to meet someone who was being held here.

"Do you think we'll really get to see her, though? I admit it's going incredibly well so far, but..." I asked Siesta as we followed a corrections officer through the building.

We'd tried to meet this prisoner many times before, but they'd never granted our requests for an interview.

"Yes. As long as we've got this, it's a sure thing." Siesta flashed the notebook that marked her as a Tuner. The Federation Government had officially issued it yesterday.

"...I see. This'll be the first time in a year, then."

We walked down some stairs, and down more stairs, until we finally reached the deepest part of the basement: a small, completely sealed steel room.

With a dull noise, a heavy shutter retracted to the side, revealing the figure behind the bars. A woman was sitting there with her chin in her hand. She had the eyes of someone who would kill anyone—even a god.

"You've got fifteen minutes," the corrections officer said, then left us.

Taking a deep breath, I called the name of the woman in the cage.

"It's been a long time, Ms. Fuubi."

◆ Because everyone had their own justice

"Hey, you damn kid, it's been a while. Did they finally arrest you, too?"

She looked at me with the hyper-focused eyes of a beast stalking its prey. Was her red hair colored like the blood of the criminals she had executed in the name of justice? She had several former titles.

For example, former police officer, and former Assassin—Fuubi Kase.

Now, she was incarcerated here as a criminal.

"I didn't get arrested. Sorry for never living up to your expectations," I said, bowing my head in a patently fake way.

Ms. Fuubi narrowed her eyes, then gave a smile that didn't go past her lips. Our positions and situations might have changed, but she definitely hadn't.

"Fuubi, what are you doing now?"

When Siesta asked her about her lifestyle, Ms. Fuubi snorted. "What does it look like I'm doing? They even exempted me from prison labor, so I've got nothing to do but strength training."

So was that the reason behind the murderous hostility? Now that she mentioned it, Ms. Fuubi hadn't become gaunt—if anything, she was more toned than before. Although her abs were hidden beneath her clothes, I suspected she might have found a way to get the fabled twelve-pack.

"So hey, you chose this one as your legal wife, huh?" Ms. Fuubi asked me, shooting Siesta a glance.

"It's not like that. Nagisa's just busy with something else right now."

"Uh, I didn't mention her name, did I?"

...I'd fallen for the oldest trick in the book.

"And? What brings you to this dump?" She raked her fingers through her hair, which was a whole lot longer now.

"Well, actually..."

I told Ms. Fuubi about the Federation Government official killings Noel had told us about yesterday. Siesta took a few reference documents out of her bag and passed them through the bars. They were copies of reports on the unknown crisis; the Federation Government had sent them over this morning.

"Why would you people tell me about this?"

Ms. Fuubi skimmed through them, getting the gist of things, then gave us a piercing look. *"Did you think this was my doing again?"*

I didn't have a prompt response for that. About fifteen seconds passed in silence.

"Unfortunately, even I can't kill people from a jail cell." Fuubi Kase broke the silence herself. "Maybe you were hoping I'd give you some sort of hint, either as a former cop or somebody who once pulled off something similar, but you've come to the wrong person. You're missing a lot of intel here."

I should've known. Ms. Fuubi shoved the documents back at us. A whole lot of them had been redacted by the Federation Government.

"Apparently the locations where the officials were killed are confidential, so they can't tell us." Flipping through the documents, Siesta gave a little sigh.

The places where the incidents had occurred, the times and dates, the code names of the murdered officials—all of it was censored. The only thing we knew was that there had already been thirteen victims.

The Federation Government ruled the world from the shadows, and I could understand why they'd keep such a tight lid on information. Even so, if they were going to make Siesta and Nagisa proxy Ace Detectives so they could investigate this, you'd think they'd be a little more cooperative.

"It's like they aren't seriously planning to have you investigate it," I said. A little irritated, I thought back to yesterday. Unlike all the other officials we'd met, Noel had seemed reasonable.

"Sorry I can't help. Is that all you needed?" Ms. Fuubi stretched lazily, starting to retreat to the back of the cell.

"No—there's another reason we're here." When I called her back, Ms. Fuubi stopped where she was, although she looked as if she probably had a few choice words for me.

"I just wanted to see you, Ms. Fuubi."

I'd been worried about her, all this time.

She gazed back at me steadily. There was an emotion in her eyes that I couldn't read.

She'd been arrested about a year ago, right after the end of the Great Cataclysm.

Since the world had attained lasting peace, the Federation Government had decided to dismantle the Tuner system. As the Assassin, Fuubi Kase had stained her hands with all sorts of dark deeds, and no sooner had she lost her privileged position than they'd decided to jail her.

To put it bluntly, she'd been charged with treason. The pretext was that she'd killed a Federation Government official, but there was no telling whether that was actually true. In any case, the higher-ups had decided that Fuubi Kase's excessive meting out of justice made her a dangerous element.

"Are you okay with this?" Siesta asked her.

Did she think it was fair that the government had decided to lock her up?

"One era's terrorist is another's celebrated revolutionary. You hear that one all the time." Ms. Fuubi turned to face us. "What happened to me is the same thing—or the reverse, that's all. I steeled myself for this to happen the day I took on the Assassin's mission." Somehow, the look on her face seemed clear and refreshed. "I may not look like it, but I'm a cop before anything else. If the world is peaceful and its citizens are happy now, then that's fine. I couldn't ask for more." Her expression softened.

"But Ms. Fuubi, didn't you say you wanted to get to the top?" When I'd first heard her say that, I'd assumed she wanted to climb the ranks as a police officer. But when I thought about it later, I realized what she'd really meant was—

"Kimizuka." Ms. Fuubi almost never said my name. Quietly, she shook her head. "I already have my answer. I joined the force in order to get it. This peaceful world is enough for me."

Come to think of it, when had it been? I'd asked Ms. Fuubi why she'd wanted to be a police officer before. Had it been a year ago? Right before the Great Cataclysm? ...What had that been about? That had been a pretty important conversation, I think.

"Still, some mysterious enemy's going around killing the ones who shoved me in here, huh? I see. That's a nice, peaceful world."

Ms. Fuubi smirked. Was she deliberately putting on an evil act?

However, she'd said she had nothing to do with this incident.

I believed her. I didn't have a choice.

"It's kind of noisy." She looked absently up at the ceiling.

Siesta seemed to have picked up on something as well; she cupped her ears, listening carefully. Was something happening above this underground cell, in the area where the regular prisoners were housed?

"That knack of yours is still going strong."

"It's a coincidence, seriously."

Please let it be a coincidence. Siesta and I exchanged looks, then turned on our heels. If the detective and her assistant were here, they couldn't just ignore trouble.

"You weren't wrong," Siesta said, stopping for a moment. "The justice of Fuubi Kase, Assassin, wasn't wrong, either."

I couldn't see her face as she said this, nor Ms. Fuubi's.

However, I knew the detective was right.

◆ That back, for the first time in seven years

"...What is this?"

When we'd climbed the stairs and opened the door leading up from the basement, what we saw stopped us in our tracks.

The prison was built around a central well. On every floor—first, second, and third—all the barred cell doors stood open. The prisoners were loose. Men in dull-colored prison uniforms raced across catwalk-like corridors and hallways.

"Assistant, hide," Siesta told me.

Ducking behind an open cell door, we took in the situation. The prisoners definitely weren't fleeing from the guards. After all, the guards were fleeing, too.

Who were they running from? The answer to that one was obvious.

It was the guy who was brandishing a snake-sword that whipped around like a living creature.

"Where is he?! Where?!" the big guy screamed, lashing out at everything in reach with that strange weapon.

The sword writhed, growing and shrinking at will. It stretched to two meters, then three, slashing through cell bars and destroying stone walls. Its twisting form was almost like...

"—A tentacle." The words were out of my mouth before I realized I was going to say them.

"Look closer, Assistant. It's not." Siesta pointed at the distant enemy.

The snake-sword wasn't growing from his ear or shoulder. While his sleeve hid it from view, he was probably holding it like a regular weapon.

Maybe because we'd just heard about something similar from the Federation Government yesterday, I'd reflexively linked this to a past experience.

"Does that mean we've already ruled him out as the culprit behind the government official killings?"

"I…think so. I can't swear that he has no connection to them, though."

In other words, we'd coincidentally happened to run into a guy like this, now of all times…?

"Still, this is perfect." Siesta sounded rather cheerful. "It's a little like that other time. It'll make for a great comeback battle."

When I glanced at her, she was wearing her usual dress. "Hey, changing scenes are special. If you're going to change, check with me first and do it right."

"That's the first setup joke you've fed me in a while. I was just thinking if our comedy skills got any rustier, we should probably disband."

"Your definition of 'business partners' is very broad… Forget that, Siesta, how are you going to stop that guy?"

"I'd like to start by shutting down that odd snake-sword of his, but…"

I could predict the rest of that sentence: We didn't have any weapons that could do that.

Now that Siesta was working as a proxy Ace Detective, she was licensed to carry a weapon. However, this was a prison. They hadn't let us take guns to our interview with Ms. Fuubi.

"Assistant, this way."

Inching closer to the enemy, we sized up the situation.

The prisoners were still running around and screaming, but the man with the snake-sword wasn't going out of his way to chase them.

"So he's not attacking at random?"

If this wasn't indiscriminate slaughter, the criminal had to have a clear objective.

"I just had a great idea." Siesta smacked her palm with her fist.

"You're a detective, all right. I knew I could count on you. Specifically what will we be doing?"

"First, you cling to that snake-sword and keep the guy from moving. Then I'll get in close and punch him in the gut."

"Don't ever call yourself the Ace Detective again."

Her instincts had gotten way too dull over the past year. Actually, no—this was basically how things had been before, too.

"After giving it some serious thought, maybe we should ask the criminal what he wants first."

"I wish you'd started with the serious thought, but yeah, I'm on board with that."

Why had he broken into the prison and started swinging that weapon around? Before we even had to ask, he gave us the answer.

"That bastard killed my little sister, and I'm gonna end him personally."

...I'd heard that one before. From Bat, a pseudohuman we'd fought ages ago. I remembered how he'd looked, lashing that snakelike tentacle around at ten thousand meters.

Either way, this criminal was out for revenge. That was why he was looking for his sworn enemy and completely ignoring unrelated prisoners.

In that case... I made eye contact with Siesta, then picked up a uniform cap dropped by a fleeing guard and tugged it onto my head. I didn't have time to actually change clothes, but maybe my suit would be enough to fool him.

"You do have that nondescript face. It's perfect for passing yourself off as somebody else."

"Watch it. I'll make you cool your heels in a disciplinary cell for two hours," I said, pretending to be a guard.

I walked over to the big guy. He was still swinging his weapon around, but it didn't take him long to notice me. He narrowed his eyes, watching to see what I'd do.

I inhaled slightly, then got started. "The person you're looking for isn't here."

The snake-sword paused in midair. However, the man's eyes stayed locked on me. "No, he's in here. He's been here for the past ten years."

"Yeah, I meant you're a little late." My mouth had gone dry, but I went on. "He got sick and died a month ago." The guy's beast-like eyes widened. "That means your enemy's not on this planet anymore. You can't take him out with that weapon."

I was making it all up, of course. In my heart, I begged the criminal the guy was targeting: *Please have made a run for it already. At least don't be dumb enough to step forward and say it was you.*

Wearing my best poker face, I waited for his decision.

"That's a lie." A few meters ahead of me, a dark light smoldered in the man's eyes. "This ain't logic. I can feel my enemy's nearby, and I don't need a special ability to do it. You're not gonna make me doubt it with your words."

In the next instant, the snake-sword stopped hesitating and flew straight at me.

"…! What, you've decided I'm hostile now, too?"

Just before that attack nailed me, though, something crashed into the enemy's blade and knocked it off course.

"Yes, that really isn't a pseudohuman." It was Siesta. She'd flung her ballpoint pen at him like a spear, blocking the attack. "That snake-sword isn't physically part of him. It's just a dangerous mechanical weapon."

"Apparently. He seems really mad, though."

The enemy glared at us. Then his blade lashed out at us like a whip.

"Assistant!"

Siesta grabbed me and jumped. The snake-sword gouged a big chunk of concrete out of the floor, right where we'd been standing. One hit from that thing would take us out instantly.

"That wasn't a bad strategy."

"Yeah, but it was a bit too simplistic. I guess nobody would give up a long-cherished ambition that easily."

As we talked, we kept evading the enemy's attacks.

That said, Siesta was literally carrying my weight. I'd become an adult and grown a bit, but there was really no way around this. It was all about dividing the labor appropriately.

"This takes me back," Siesta whispered. "It was like this seven years ago, too."

Yeah, it had been. The first time I'd met Siesta, at ten thousand meters.

That was where I'd learned that the world had some powerful enemies, and that there was a great detective who fought them. Come to think of it, we'd had a rough time against that enemy's snakelike attacks, too, and then Siesta had said exactly what she was saying now:

"If I just had a weapon or something…"

Unfortunately, I didn't have an attaché case on standby today.

"Still, I guess we managed to buy some time."

"We did. She's right around the corner."

When she reached a certain spot, Siesta set me down, then froze. Once again, the snake-sword closed in on us. We hadn't given up, though.

The detective was already fully prepared.

"Siesta! Catch!"

The musket Nagisa Natsunagi had thrown from the upper floor landed right in Siesta's hands.

That had been the other detective's job today. She was fully prepared, too: She'd gone to pick up this weapon from the former Men in Black.

"Brilliant work, Nagisa."

With a single bullet, the whole incident was over.

That formidable back was proof that the Ace Detective had returned.

◆ What I can do to end this story

The next day, Noel de Lupwise visited the Shirogane Detective Agency as a client.

We'd contacted her to tell her there'd been a development in the government official killings case the previous evening, and unexpectedly, she'd come to see us in person.

"Tell me at once, please: What new information have you found regarding the unknown crisis?"

Siesta and Nagisa sat side by side on the sofa, while Noel sat across from them, gazing at them seriously.

…Where was I? Making tea for the three of them. That's an assistant's job, you know.

"Before we get started on the main topic, Noel, may I ask you a question?" I set a cup of black tea in front of her. "I'm really curious about your outfit. Are those your casual clothes?"

"My outfit? Yes, I changed before I came. I didn't want to seem discourteous."

Noel was wearing an extremely ruffly, highly embellished black dress. Was it one of those Gothic Lolita things? With her European features, it was a good look for her; she really did look like a doll. But what had brought this on?

"When in Rome, do as the Romans do. You have a similar proverb in Japan, don't you? I've studied Japanese fashion in addition to traditional Japanese dress."

"Where did you study to end up with those results? Did you visit a subculture hotspot or something?"

"At the café I visited yesterday, all the waitresses were dressed like this."

"That's just a themed café. You picked a hyper-unique place to visit."

Geez, so she could have showed up as a maid or a ninja? Her commitment was laudable, but I was concerned that someday, she might be tricked when the stakes were higher.

"Noel, are you wearing a different perfume this time?" Siesta asked abruptly.

"I'm not wearing perfume. That's odd..." Noel sniffed at her own arm, trying to pick up her scent. *She looks like a small animal*, I thought, gazing at her. I pulled a chair over and sat down.

All right, that was enough small talk. On to the main topic. When I cleared my throat, Noel got the hint and asked her question again. "Could you tell me about the development in the case?"

Siesta, Nagisa, and I exchanged looks. After that incident at the prison yesterday, the three of us had talked it over and come up with a certain theory.

"Right up front, I should clarify that the development wasn't in regard to the case itself. It's more fundamental than that," I said, speaking for the detectives.

Noel cocked her head as if she didn't understand.

That was weird, though. She had to know.

"When the Federation Government gave Siesta and Nagisa authority as Ace Detectives, *it wasn't actually so they could investigate the government official killings, was it?*"

Several things had made us suspect as much. The first had been those copied documents they'd sent us, which were supposed to provide details on the killings. No matter how hard we tried, there was no way to investigate using information that had been censored that heavily. They'd said the situation was urgent, but they really didn't seem serious about their request.

Second, the setup was just too neat. Yesterday, right as we were at the prison visiting Ms. Fuubi, an enemy who reminded us of a certain pseudo-human had attacked. In another bit of exquisite timing, Nagisa had picked up the musket from a nearby Man in Black, and Siesta had used it to take down the attacker, completing a job that was a whole lot like what the Ace Detective used to do.

It was all too perfect. We didn't think the Federation Government had actually sent the guy with the snake-sword, but they might have known more or less what was going to happen around then, and also deduced that, if they gave us Tuner notebooks, the first thing we'd do was use that authority to get an interview with Fuubi Kase. The government had intentionally put us on a collision course with that man.

"Why would we do that?" Noel asked, once I'd explained.

"To make us Ace Detectives in both word and deed again, correct?" Siesta said. "Thanks to that, I'm completely in the mood for it now." She gave a small sigh.

This was how it had worked: Two days ago, they'd told us multiple government officials had been killed, and called this an unknown crisis. Then they'd given us information that suggested the incident was related to a global crisis the Ace Detective had taken care of. That meant Siesta and Nagisa had practically been forced to agree to investigate, since it was portrayed as cleanup for an old crisis.

At that point, Siesta and Nagisa had only been carrying out the Ace Detective's work as temporary proxies, but then yesterday's incident had happened. By making them encounter and resolve an incident similar to one they'd lived through previously, the Federation Government had attempted to reawaken Siesta and Nagisa's instincts as Ace Detectives and bring back those old feelings.

That meant the government official killings had only been bait to get the two of them interested in the role again. We didn't know whether the crisis was entirely manufactured, but Siesta thought the elements Noel had told us about that sounded deliberate—such as the "tentacle fragments"— had probably been falsified.

"...In that case, why would the Federation Government wish to return the two of you to the post of Ace Detective? Are you saying we had a reason to go to such lengths?"

"We called you here today to ask about that," Nagisa responded. "What is the job you really want us to do? Something's coming that will require an Ace Detective, isn't there?"

Silence fell. Siesta lifted her cup of tea to her lips, and the quiet *clink* when she returned it to its saucer was the only sound in the room. The ball was in Noel's court now, and all we could do was wait.

"*Corretto.* That's right."

But when the answer finally came, it wasn't from Noel.

A man had opened the agency door and come in. Raising his hat slightly, he gave us a smile that was framed by prominent white whiskers.

"Oh, I knew it," Siesta murmured next to me, as if it all made sense now. "I had a feeling you were behind this, Bruno."

"It's been a long time, you three." Our visitor looked at each of us in turn, apparently pleased to see us.

This was Bruno Belmondo, the former Information Broker. It was the first time we'd seen each other since the Great Cataclysm last year.

"Bruno? Why are you...?" Unlike Siesta, Nagisa looked puzzled.

Still smiling, the old man walked over with the aid of a cane and took a seat across from us, next to Noel. He gently laid a hand on her head. "You've been a great help to my granddaughter."

Noel's expression softened slightly.

"She's your granddaughter? But your last names..."

Noel's last name was Lupwise. Bruno's was Belmondo.

"Yes. As a matter of fact, I was adopted by the Belmondo family for a time," Noel explained. As she went on, she occasionally exchanged glances with Bruno. "Due to a certain situation, that's no longer true, but

Grandfather raised me for quite a while. I only returned to my current family a year ago."

In other words, Noel had been a Belmondo longer than she had been a Lupwise? This was apparently news to Siesta as well; she nodded slightly, watching the two of them. Still, why were we being introduced at a time like this?

"Perhaps it's my age. I've wanted to boast to you about my treasure for a while now."

"Grandfather, are you drunk? That's embarrassing; please don't." Although Noel had always been calm and collected with us, her lips were moving slightly now in an awkward, restless way.

Bruno grinned at his granddaughter. Then his eyes went to Siesta. "However, you seem to have realized that I was behind Noel."

"I just had a feeling," Siesta told him. "Noel smelled a bit like you today. Cologne, brandy, and the smell of a wind that's spent a hundred years traveling."

Bruno's eyebrows twitched as if she'd surprised him. Then he laughed, stroking his chin. "Indeed, she wouldn't have noticed that."

That was just like the Ace Detective: She had a nose sharper than a wild Cerberus's.

"Well, Bruno? If you're here, does that mean you're planning to tell us what's really going on?" I got the conversation back on topic. Why did the Federation Government want to make Siesta and Nagisa Ace Detectives again so badly that they'd sent us on this chase? If Bruno was the one behind Noel, explaining this had to be his job.

"First, about your premise." Bruno's expression turned serious. "The theory you set out a moment ago is basically correct. The things that happened around you for the past few days were necessary in order to make the two detectives Tuners again. The unknown crisis wasn't a complete fabrication, though. It will actually occur, later on."

"Do we know when?" Nagisa asked. Since he was the former Information Broker, she seemed to think he probably would.

"On the day of the Ritual of Sacred Return."

...Oh, was that it? An occasion that would attract the Federation

Government, the former Tuners, and important people from around the world. If an unknown entity really did have a grudge against the world, striking on that day would be logical.

"Is this 'unknown crisis' a new enemy? What are they?"

"*It refers to a messenger from a certain sanctuary.*" Bruno narrowed his eyes, lowering his voice slightly. "That sanctuary is said to be an unknown nation or continent, or perhaps an unobserved satellite. It's the one place where the Federation Government can't interfere. However, it occasionally accesses the Federation Government unilaterally, using a transmission method modern science can't explain."

Was he saying there was still an undiscovered nation somewhere on the planet? Granted, since I knew of life-forms such as Seed, who had lived on an unobserved satellite, I couldn't deny the possibility.

"We call this undetectable territory 'Another Eden.'"

Bruno coughed lightly a few times. "Grandfather," Noel said, gently rubbing his back.

"...I've heard a little about that. I was told the sanctuary's messengers have tried to attack the world several times before." Siesta thought hard, one finger on her chin. "Then you mean the next attack will occur on the day of the Ritual of Sacred Return? And that's what you're calling the 'unknown crisis'?"

"That's right, Miss Siesta." Bruno was still coughing, so Noel responded for him. "Just the other day, Another Eden made contact with us. During the transmission, they announced that they would attack on that day. They also said they would hear our answer at the Ritual."

"Your answer? Are they negotiating with the Federation Government over something?"

"Yes, Mr. Kimihiko. To put it simply, they wish to make a certain treaty with us. However..." Noel faltered. Apparently, the negotiations weren't going well.

As a result, the messengers of Another Eden had resorted to force, over and over. This time was no exception.

"By the way, what is this treaty?" Nagisa asked. I'd been wondering about that myself. The Federation Government was secretive, and I suspected it wouldn't be that easy to find out; however, Noel told us readily.

In short, it was a peace treaty between the Federation Government and Another Eden. However, as a condition of the treaty, the sanctuary's messengers had demanded the transfer of a certain thing in the possession of the Federation Government which had been declared a global classified matter. The government had said they didn't know what Another Eden was talking about and rejected the request, and as such, the treaty was still in limbo.

"Therefore, right now, all we can do is prepare." Once he'd recovered from his coughing fit, Bruno spoke emphatically. "In roughly two weeks, the unknown crisis will occur at the Ritual of Sacred Return. In the time that remains, we would like you to learn as much as you can of the world, and to steel yourselves. Be ready to throw yourselves into the horrors of war once more."

"And that's why you want Siesta and Nagisa to be Ace Detectives again?"

"Exactly. I am old, and what I can do is limited. I want to acquire as many comrades as I can."

I knew it. This was what the events of the past few days had meant. What did Siesta and Nagisa think of all this?

"Let's do it." Siesta answered before anyone else. I'd known she would agree, after I'd seen her with her musket yesterday.

"Yes. After all, we're detectives." Having known Nagisa since she was still a proxy detective, I knew full well how much pride she took in the job.

I shot another glance at the two detectives. Their eyes were fixed on tomorrow. That meant there was only one answer I could give.

"I'm your assistant. Take me wherever you want to go."

If the year after the cataclysm was a peaceful epilogue...

Then let's go find the future—the credits that will let us keep those ordinary days.

A certain day at a certain detective agency

Nine in the morning.

That was around the time days at the Shirogane Detective Agency began, at least when we didn't have class.

The agency was on the second floor of a mixed-use building. When I unlocked the door and turned the knob, I was greeted by the familiar sight of the office.

I opened the curtains, then booted up my computer. After taking a quick look to make sure none of the new emails were urgent, I started to do some basic cleaning.

That said, since both the chief and the detective were neat people, the office stayed pretty clean anyway. I ran a broom over the floor, and I was starting to organize documents when the door opened.

"Good morning. You're early, Kimihiko." Nagisa Natsunagi came in, yawning a little. She hung her overcoat on the coat rack, then sat down at her desk and stretched.

"Didn't get enough sleep? I bet you spent all night watching foreign dramas again."

"No, my lab had a drinking party that went late yesterday. The professor stayed, too, so it was hard to duck out early."

"We're in the same lab, right? How come nobody invited me?"

Did the grad students and the professor just not know I existed or something? Would I actually manage to graduate? A little uneasy, I sat down at my desk as well. "I guess I'll get to work."

Nine thirty AM.

Now that two employees were present, we gradually got down to business...or that's what should have happened.

"Have we gotten any new cases?"

"Just marketing emails from a printer rental place."

"So it's the same as usual. I wonder if we'll get paid this month..." Nagisa slumped apathetically.

We hadn't gotten any proper cases since that infidelity investigation, aka "the stalker incident." That was partly inevitable, though.

The Shirogane Detective Agency didn't have a website. The only way we advertised was by posting a flyer on the bulletin board at the train station, and most people probably didn't even know we existed.

"Well, if that's the chief's policy, we can't complain."

According to Siesta, the service industry was all about assigning the right jobs to the right people. There were already plenty of places where regular people could ask for help and get it. She said our job was to be a place that would help the irregular types.

"I'll think I'll make a shopping run," Nagisa announced. "I'm bored. Do we need anything?"

"Snacks to serve clients with tea, maybe? Although we'll just end up eating them ourselves."

"True," Nagisa said with a laugh. Standing up, she grabbed her coat.

"Want me to go with? I can carry stuff."

"Mm. If you're there, something weird will happen to me, so no thanks."

"Not fair."

Nagisa left, and I was on my own again. The chief still hadn't come by yet.

Ten AM.

I made myself some coffee, and when I got back to my desk, an email had come in.

It was from Noel de Lupwise, the Federation Government official. She hadn't contacted us since her visit two days ago. The email had a link for a video chat, and I got my headset out and responded to the call.

"Good morning, Mr. Kimihiko."

On the screen, Noel was primly dressed in a traditional Japanese kimono.

She nodded to me. She seemed to be in her room; I could see European-style furnishings behind her. Had she gone back home? (She'd said she was from France, right?) If so… "It's the middle of the night over there, isn't it? You're sure this is an okay time for you?"

"*Yes, I still have heaps of work to get through.*"

Apparently, the Federation Government was even harder on its staff than the detective agency was.

"Well, what did you need? If you want to talk to the chief, I'll go wake her up."

Siesta was probably upstairs sleeping peacefully right about now.

"*No, that's all right. Grandfather told me how much the detective sleeps. He said she sleeps a lot, eats a lot, and she's still growing like a weed.*"

"What is she, a kid?"

While we were talking, a new email came in. This one had airplane tickets to France attached to it. They were for the Ritual of Sacred Return, ten days from now. For the Federation Government, this was unusually generous.

"*I would like you to read through this email. We're also reserving a hotel for you. Do you have any requests regarding the type of room?*"

"Nah, anything's fine. We don't care if you put all three of us in one room."

Back when I was wandering around with Siesta, just having a place where I could stretch my legs out and sleep was plenty.

"*You three really are close, aren't you? Which of the two are you courting, Mr. Kimihiko?*"

"If I were dating one of them, we wouldn't be sleeping three to a room. What kind of ethics do you think I have?"

"*It's all right. I'll put together a list of countries and regions that allow polygamy for you right away.*"

"I know you're a government official; you don't have to show off," I retorted.

Noel dropped her cool, blank expression in order to smile just a little. "*You three really do seem like family, though. I envy that.*"

"Like family, huh? As categories go, 'colleagues' is still more accurate."

Besides, if we were talking about family, Noel also had… I was about to say it, but instead of finishing my sentence, I decided to go with something else. "What are your living arrangements like now?"

"I've reassumed the Lupwise family name, but I live alone... To be honest, my memories of that house aren't very good ones."

"...I see. You still see Bruno, though, right?"

"Yes, we dine together and talk about unimportant things once a month, every month."

Considering their respective positions, they probably couldn't talk about work most of the time. Bruno had been the Information Broker for much of his life, and he said he almost never shared his knowledge. Even members of the government or his family wouldn't be exceptions to that rule.

"I don't know whether Grandfather really enjoys those meals. We simply make small talk."

"I doubt Bruno would meet you every month if he wasn't enjoying it, don't you think?"

"I...hope that's the case," Noel said evasively, averting her eyes.

"Still, yeah, you never do know what the other person's feeling, do you?"

Noel tilted her head slightly. *"You don't either, Mr. Kimihiko?"*

Nope. I didn't know what Nagisa and Siesta were actually thinking now.

"You can only vaguely guess what somebody else is feeling from memory and the time you've spent with them. No matter how much you think about it, you ultimately have to let your ego make the call."

For example, *They must be thinking along these lines, so if I do this, it'll probably make them happy.* People are self-centered creatures, and that's the only way we can live. That's why we at least need to build relationships that can survive the clashes of our egos.

"Yes, that's right. I'm sorry; that was an odd thing to say." Noel looked just a little happy. *"And thank you... If I'd had someone like you in my family, I think I could have held my head a bit higher."*

"Is that a dignitary joke, too?" I asked.

"That's a good question," Noel said, smiling slightly.

"I'm sure you've got a lot going on, but for now, we need to focus on the Ritual of Sacred Return and stay alert."

We had ten days before the unknown crisis was supposed to occur. In the time we had left, we needed to figure out what we could do.

"For starters, could you send us the guest list for the Ritual? We'd like to get a handle on who's going to be attending, just in case. If you can't reveal information about people connected to the Federation Government, then just information on the people who aren't would be fine."

"*Very well. I'll send it right over. At the moment, we're working to contact the other former Tuners. As Grandfather said, he wants to have as many comrades as possible.*"

Right—the more allies we had, the better we'd feel. After arranging to contact each other again, we ended our chat.

"Huh. You worry about some surprisingly delicate things, Kimi."

I'd thought I was alone in the room. But when I turned around, I saw Siesta standing there.

"How much of that did you hear?" I asked.

"I came in at the part where you were worrying about love."

There hadn't been any such scene. Probably.

"If you're wondering, I hear there are many polygamous nations in West Africa."

"Huh. Is that right? What I am wondering is, when and why did you check into that?"

"...I just know it as general knowledge." With a rather pointed cough, Siesta crossed to her own desk. As she booted up her computer, she commented, "I don't think you're wrong, Kimi."

I knew we were on a different subject now, but I had no idea what she was trying to say. I waited for her next words, and then—

"After all, there's a detective right here who was set in motion by one boy's ego."

Siesta's expression didn't change at all, but she was definitely looking at me.

"I see," I murmured. I took another sip of my coffee, which hadn't quite gone cold yet.

"I'm hooome— Oh, Siesta's up." Just then, Nagisa came back, carrying a shopping bag.

"I've been up for ages. I was just late because I took a shower and did some reading and had my tea and watched a movie."

"Ah, mm-hmm, sure. Never mind the excuses." Parrying Siesta with well-practiced ease, Nagisa set the things she'd bought out on the desk. "I picked up some yummy-looking bread at the station. Want to split it three ways?"

Ten thirty AM.

It would be a while longer before we actually got down to business.

Chapter 2

◆ If that's an idol's job...

Five days after Bruno and Noel's visit, because school was still on winter break, Nagisa and I went to a certain artist's concert.

The venue was the National Stadium, which had been designed by a famous architect.

The stadium was surrounded by trees, and it really felt as though we were in the middle of a forest: Nature and the artificial had been joined in perfect harmony. On that stage, Japan's most famous idol was giving the final performance of her national tour.

"Farther, farther, out beyond the skies, our hearts will always be our allies... ♪"

The concert was near its midpoint. The idol on the central stage was turning up the heat, whipping up the excitement of the audience. We stood at the back of the standing room section, waving back at her with a pink-colored light stick in each hand.

"The sign is hope, shout out that motto louder, louder... ♪"

Thunderous cheers and shouts rocked the venue.

However, I just kept silently offering my light sticks to the stage. Yelling wasn't the only way to cheer someone on. As her fan, sometimes it was important to watch over her quietly from the back rows...

"Y-you're crying." Next to me, Nagisa was staring at me like I was a total weirdo. "That other time, you yelled like crazy. I think that might have been healthier, don't you?"

"Just look at Yui-nya, all grown up. Who wouldn't cry?"

"What exactly are you to Yui?" Nagisa sighed and rolled her eyes. I didn't have time to bother with her now, though.

"Thank you so much, everyone! That was *You-Colored Gimmick!*"

Finishing her song, Yui-nya—aka Saikawa—waved at her fans. I returned the gesture with a little wave of my own… Oh, hey! Our eyes just met!

She was looking at me! I'm positive!

"When Yui grew up, are you sure you didn't switch places with her and regress, Kimihiko?"

Right after that, Saikawa launched into a talk segment, carrying herself with even more confidence than before.

"Although I guess it does feel as if she's gone somewhere out of reach." As Nagisa gazed at Yui, she seemed to be looking at something very far away.

Yui Saikawa, idol and current high school student.

She'd been in middle school when we met, and now she was in her second year of high school. Her popularity hadn't suffered at all in the meantime; she was more successful than ever now. She was working as an actress in the domestic film industry, too, and she was nailing overseas performances one after another.

She was the idol whose tickets were hardest to get. Nagisa and I had only been accommodated because we were connected. Siesta had wanted to come, but then she'd said she had work today and holed up at the agency instead.

"Even for fan club members, the win rate for concert tickets is under five percent. It's gotten even harder to see her in person."

"Yes. More importantly, Kimihiko, I'd never heard that you were in Yui's fan club."

Hadn't I mentioned that? I've been a member for three years. A group bulletin shows up every month.

"Well then, we were really lucky to be invited today."

"As a genuine fan, I do feel a little guilty for taking a shortcut."

"I mean, it's not like we came to the concert for fun in the first place."

Yeah, I know that. There's a rather serious conversation waiting after this.

But until then, at least, I thought I'd bask in Super Idol Saikawa's catchy, crazy world.

About two hours later, when we visited Yui Saikawa's dressing room as scheduled, we found her drinking tea and taking a breather after a successful concert.

"Oh!" When she saw us, she jumped to her feet and ran over, her eyes sparkling. A little nervous, I spread my arms, bracing for her to fling herself into them—

"Nagisa, I missed you!"

—but Saikawa dived into Nagisa's arms instead.

"Yui, it's been ages!"

Next to me, Nagisa was hugging Saikawa close and spinning around and around.

Yeah, this was about what I expected.

"Oh, Kimizuka. Hello." Saikawa poked her head out of Nagisa's arms.

"That was on purpose, wasn't it? You can't have done that by accident." I gave her a look. Saikawa giggled.

"Actually, Saikawa, why are you dressed for school?"

Now that the concert was over, for some reason, she was wearing her high school uniform.

"I hadn't seen you in a long time, Kimizuka, so I was trying to think of the very best outfit for the occasion, and this is what I came up with. How does it look?" Saikawa plucked her uniform ribbon up between her fingertips, showing it off.

Yes, Saikawa in uniform was a novel sight, but… "So does that mean you were actually looking forward to seeing me, too?"

"…Oh, shut up. I can't stand people who can't read the mood." Saikawa averted her face, snubbing me, and went back to Nagisa.

Why is Nagisa getting all the attention? Should I have been born as a girl or something?

"Honestly, you haven't changed a bit." Someone in the dressing room was watching me coldly. "Nothing's more unsightly than jealousy in a man, Kimihiko."

The girl who'd spoken had been making tea for Saikawa, and she looked exactly like a younger Siesta.

"Gender has nothing to do with how jealous people get, Noches."

Noches gave a thin smile that didn't make it past her lips. "Everyone says we should care less about gender, but it's actually just getting stricter, isn't it?"

The girl in the classic maid outfit lambasted social conditions with extremely unrobotic sarcasm. In another few years, the world might be wanting android-blindness, too.

"So you're with Saikawa when she's away from home, too, huh?"

"Yes. As the Saikawa household's head maid, it's only natural that I act as Miss Yui's guard."

Noches had begun working for the Saikawa family a year ago. While her former mistress Siesta slept, she'd been Siesta's main caretaker. When Siesta woke up, Noches had been released from her mission, and now she was working as Saikawa's head maid.

"You're keeping as busy as ever, then."

"Yes, just tending to the mansion and the garden every day takes until sundown. Why do trees grow so quickly?" Noches said. "Granted, I am doing this because I want to." A year ago, the one who'd released her from her mission had been Siesta herself. Siesta had said Noches could live as she chose, but...

"I really do like serving people."

Noches was still working as a maid voluntarily. That had to be a good thing.

"Not much has changed with you, either, I see." Noches was gazing at Saikawa and Nagisa, who were chatting animatedly. From what I heard, she and Siesta swapped information every so often, so she was very familiar with our everyday lives.

"Siesta and Nagisa fight a lot, though."

Then, thirty minutes later, they'd be friends again and chatting up a storm, as if it was some sort of girls-only party. Thinking about those times made me sigh.

"That sounds like fun," said Noches.

"It's tiring, that's what it is."

"I meant for you, Kimihiko." Unexpectedly, Noches gazed at me. "You sound as if you're having fun."

"...Yeah, I guess," I said, in a voice low enough that no one else could hear. You had to be pretty clever to hide anything from Noches.

"Now then, shall we move on to the main topic?" Noches said, and Saikawa and Nagisa stopped chatting and came over to join us.

"You have something to tell Miss Yui, don't you?"

I nodded, then gave a brief explanation of the unknown crisis. I'd spotted Saikawa's name on the guest list for the Ritual of Sacred Return that Noel had sent over. Yui Saikawa had worked with us to stop the Great Cataclysm; that was probably what had earned her a place at the ceremony.

"I see. So that's going to happen a week from now..." After I'd filled her in, Saikawa started thinking hard.

"I hadn't decided whether to attend the ceremony yet, actually. I have an overseas performance a week from now..."

"I see. Right after the end of your national tour. That's rough," I commiserated.

"It's fun, though," she said, flashing her white teeth in a grin.

For a little while, we were all silent. Saikawa was the one who started the conversation back up. "The rest of you are getting involved with the world again, aren't you?"

I almost told her, *You're singing with the world as your stage, too*, then realized that wasn't what she meant. When Saikawa said "the world," she meant all the extraordinary stuff we'd lived through earlier.

The past year had been comparatively peaceful. However, if that unknown crisis did occur at the upcoming ceremony, we'd connect with the extraordinary again for the first time in ages.

"...What do you think I should do?" Saikawa's smile looked a little troubled. "Not long ago, the enemies on Earth were formidable. Everyone really thought we might be done for. However, Siesta and Nagisa are both here now, and we're all happy and healthy. This past year has been so much fun that it's felt like a dream."

Saikawa had spent the entire year completely out of touch with the extraordinary. Her dreams for her career as an idol singer were coming true every day. That was probably why she was hesitating now.

Personally, I was impressed that she'd stuck with us for as long as she had. Her left eye had been directly involved in the Seed incident, but she'd kept helping us try to resurrect Siesta even after we'd defeated him. And so...

"I bet it was quite a burden to carry, wasn't it?" Maybe I'd leaned too hard on her kindness.

"A burden? Well..." Saikawa thought for a moment. "It was certainly heavy," she said, looking from me to Nagisa and back. For some reason, she seemed a little bashful. "As far as I'm concerned, the two of you have always, always been too heavy and important for me to carry, even if I use both hands."

Her brilliant smile reminded me of something I'd seen before.

It had happened during the Sapphire Eye incident, the case where we'd met Saikawa. On the day we'd solved it, we'd been in her dressing room after a concert, just as we were now. Back then, Nagisa's intense passion had brought us together, joining us with a bond we couldn't sever no matter what.

"You really are an idol, Yui." Nagisa smiled gently at Saikawa. It sounded like she was stating the obvious, but that probably wasn't quite it. "If you say the world now is like a dream, then I'd like you to protect everyone's ordinary lives as an idol."

Right. What Nagisa was trying to tell Yui was that...

"After all, it's an idol's job to show everyone a dream, isn't it?"

Saikawa's eyes widened.

There was more than one way to be involved with the world.

Those who predicted global crises, those who fought enormous evils, those who healed the wounded, and those who protected the ordinary lives everyone hoped to return to. There was more than one way to defend what was right. And so—

"Yes, gladly!"

As Saikawa said this, she was wearing her usual pure smile.

The idol might have grown up a bit, but she was still Yui Saikawa, as large as life.

◆ A beautiful, consummate kidnapping

After that, we chatted with Saikawa and Noches for a bit, and then Nagisa and I left the stadium. Just as we were thinking about heading home for the day, I got a text from an unknown sender.

It said, *I have your precious Ace Detective.*

As soon as we saw it, Nagisa and I headed for the Shirogane Detective Agency.

"Siesta!"

We unlocked the door and burst into the office, but the white-haired detective wasn't in her usual chair at the back of the room. Our ray of hope was gone.

"...! No... Why?"

Someone had snatched Siesta.

We were too late. I dropped to my knees, and my vision went dark.

"Oh, come on! What is this, a visual novel bad ending? Get up already!" Nagisa hauled me back to my feet. "Look at this." She showed me the notebook that had been sitting on the desk. Something was written on it.

"'If you want your precious detective back, come to the top of the communications tower,' it says. So it really is a kidnapping?" I said.

"Mm... I don't think Siesta would let herself be carried off that easily." She had a point. If anything, I could see her lethally injuring the kidnapper with a counterattack. "Then, what, somebody she knew did this?"

"Right. And I bet Siesta knew she was being taken away. The kidnapper wrote this note with the ballpoint pen on the desk over there."

"Oh, you're right. You can sort of tell from the texture of the ink."

That meant the kidnapper had written their challenge to us right here, in this office, probably in Siesta's presence.

"They put the pen back in the holder, though, and I don't see any signs of a fight. That means this was premeditated, and Siesta agreed to it."

I see. Which meant the threat level was pretty low.

"Now that we know that, let's go find our precious Ace Detective. Our *'precious Ace Detective.'*"

"What's that look for? I didn't write this, okay?"

I picked up the letter the kidnapper (?) had written. The top of the communications tower, huh? "Which one, though? Red or blue?"

Japan had two famous communications towers: a venerable old red one, and a comparatively new blue one.

"What are you saying? The other day, the blue one got, you know…"

"Oh, right. So red, then."

Leaving the agency, we grabbed a taxi and headed for what was formerly the nation's tallest communications tower. Siesta wasn't there, though. Instead, taped to the glass on the observation deck, there was another note with the name of a new destination.

We got shunted around from place to place—cafés, used bookstores, churches—until well after the sky had darkened and filled up with stars. Finally, Nagisa and I found ourselves at an old amusement park. It was closed for the day, and apart from us, there wasn't a soul around.

Of course, we weren't there to have fun. In accordance with the letter's instructions, we infiltrated the service area of one of the attractions. When we removed some of the floor tiles, we found a ladder leading down to a door.

"Any day now." Weary in body and soul, I opened the iron door, and—

"Hold still, Charlie. You've got soot on your face."

"Hee-hee! Ma'am, that tickles!"

A woman in a tank top was inside, cheerfully letting Siesta clean her face with a towel.

"What are you doing, Charlie?"

"Oh, that didn't take you as long as I expected."

The woman's name was Charlotte Arisaka Anderson. She was our former companion, an agent who was active worldwide. She used her assassination techniques to save people, and I didn't even know how many scrapes she'd gotten me out of.

Charlie had weaknesses, though. For one thing, battles of wits were definitely not her forte. For another, she liked Siesta so much she'd accidentally kidnapped her, among other things. (Don't accidentally kidnap people.)

"Oh, Assistant and Nagisa. You came."

"...Sheesh. Well, I'm glad you're all right."

Come to think of it, when Charlie had chosen the phrase "precious detective," had she been speaking from her own point of view? Talk about the world's dumbest kidnapper.

"You made us take the long way around on purpose. You wanted to enjoy your alone time with Siesta."

"I have no idea what you're talking about. I was just testing you, to see whether you'd lost your edge," Charlie said, brushing me off with a vague smile. She straightened up and took the long-barreled gun that had been leaning against the wall—Siesta's musket. She began polishing it with a cloth.

"What is this place? What were you doing here, Siesta?"

My first impression of the room had been "somebody's secret base." Multiple monitors showed security footage from inside the park, and there was a worktable littered with brushes and oilcans by the wall.

"I've been having Charlie do maintenance on my gun. I'm considering having her decorate the barrel with a new floral pattern while I'm at it. What do you think?"

"I couldn't care less if I tried."

◆ The agent's two faces

"Still, what's a secret base doing here?" I asked Charlie, although my eyes stayed on the monitors. They showed Siesta and Nagisa, who'd gone off to play on the equipment. The detective had said she wanted to have some fun while she was here. I'm not saying which detective it was.

"Nobody would ever think to look for it here. That's the whole point," Charlie responded. She was cleaning up the worktable. "The enemy would never expect to find a hideout under a theme park, you know?"

"'Enemy'? Who exactly are you fighting?"

"Well, that's a good question. I don't get as many opportunities to use this place these days."

The way she phrased that made it sound as if she'd used lots of camouflaged hideouts in her work as an agent, way back when. Now she was using this one to do maintenance on Siesta's gun, which Siesta hadn't used for a while.

"Wasn't this sort of thing usually Stephen's job, though?"

Stephen Bluefield, the Inventor, was the one who'd originally made Siesta's musket. I'd assumed maintaining it would be his job as well.

"I hear he's gone missing. He was a doctor to begin with, though; he might just be focusing on medical work somewhere."

...Ah. In that case, maybe Bruno hadn't managed to get in contact with him, either.

"So Ma'am is going to be the Ace Detective again," Charlie murmured, her hands falling still. Since Siesta had asked Charlie to work on her gun, she must have explained why it was necessary... Actually, even if Siesta hadn't said anything, the agent would know about a situation like that.

"Just as a temporary proxy, but yeah." That was what Noel had promised, at least. "Are you attending the Ritual of Sacred Return, too, Charlie?"

Naturally, the agent's name had been on the guest list. I'd assumed Charlie would make up her mind without any input from me, but since we'd run into each other, it wouldn't hurt to discuss it.

"A long time ago..." Instead of answering my question, Charlie began to tell an old story. "As an agent, I was given an assignment to protect a girl in a disputed area. Her parents were both high-ranking military officers. They were likely targets for the enemy, so they wanted me to keep their daughter safe."

Charlie had never talked much about her work. She probably had a duty to keep things confidential, of course, but she also seemed to be holding back for her own reasons.

"For three weeks after that, that girl and I lived in a war zone by ourselves, evading attacks."

If Charlie felt the need to tell me about this, it was probably going somewhere. I listened quietly.

"We huddled together in a simple dugout, listening to the sound of artillery fire. Our food ran low, so we shared water and crackers with each other and desperately talked about our dreams. We kept our eyes fixed on the future, and we survived."

"That was your 'normal,' wasn't it, Charlie?" I wasn't sympathizing with her—sympathy would have meant irresponsibly denying the way she'd chosen to live. It was the last thing I should do.

"What do you think the hardest part of our escape was?"

I tried to visualize her situation. The incessant gunfire, the hunger, the sanitation issues, the mortal danger... No, Charlie would have prioritized her young charge's life over her own.

"The hardest part was that the day after we started living that way, I was informed that the girl's parents had died in combat. For the next three weeks, I kept that fact hidden from her."

That answer would only make sense to those who'd stood on a real battlefield. Charlie had lied because the girl needed hope if she was going to survive. She couldn't take that away.

"Finally, there was a cease-fire. I evacuated the girl to the embassy, and once we were there, I told her the truth. —She cried and called me a liar."

Charlie had kept her voice cool up until this point, but I could see the uncertainty growing in her emerald eyes.

You weren't wrong. But I knew that sort of superficial comfort was useless. I couldn't sympathize, much less share her feelings. All I could do was listen.

"Sorry for rambling on like this." Charlie seemed to be feeling chilly now; she shrugged into her jacket. "It's just that, sometimes, the fact that those kinds of situations were routine to me scares me. I'm weak, aren't I?" she murmured.

"All people are," I told her, and she forced a smile.

If she'd gone out of her way to tell me this, she probably wasn't sure yet. She didn't know whether she had the courage to live through any more days like that. If she attended the Ritual of Sacred Return, would it force her to deal with disasters again?

"But you all are going anyway, right?"

"Yeah. Both detectives say we are, so that's that."

"If you said you didn't want to, I bet they'd stay home for you."

"Why would I say that?" I laughed the suggestion off.

Charlie gave me a long, pointed look. "You're worried about them, aren't you?"

I didn't answer. I was watching Siesta and Nagisa on the monitors. They were laughing as they rode the merry-go-round in that dark, deserted amusement park.

"I can tell. I know what you're thinking."

That made me turn around.

"When you really loathe somebody, you know exactly what makes them tick." Charlie gave me her biggest, brightest smile.

Geez. Had there ever been a more irritating grin?

"Lying to somebody you can't stand is pretty pointless, isn't it?"

In other words, since there was no love lost between us anyway, Charlie was saying I should tell her what I really thought.

"Yeah, I'm worried," I murmured, gazing at the monitors again. "They really seem to be enjoying themselves, and...frankly, the thought that they might end up in danger again scares me so much I can't sleep. Really, it makes me wish they were there, sleeping next to me."

"Okay, that's creepy."

"Don't just cut me down like that." I cleared my throat, then tried again. "But I am uneasy. If we don't attend the Ritual of Sacred Return, though, they'll always be shackled to the Tuners. —The story won't be able to come to an end."

That meant we didn't have a choice. Not everyone gets the right to choose. We had to keep moving forward, believing that the path we walked would lead us to the credits we were hoping for.

"I see. That's all I've got to say, then," Charlie told me. "I guess I'll go play, too," she added, starting to leave the hideout.

"Just so you know, I didn't tell you what I really thought because I hate you or anything," I called after her. Nor had it been because she didn't matter. "I told you because we're comrades."

Charlie's eyes widened slightly. "I see." That was all she said as she turned away.

In the moment she turned, I caught a glimpse of her profile. I thought

I saw a vaguely happy smile there, but it had to have been my imagination. Right?

◆ A night sky at ten thousand meters

When I opened my eyes, I was up on a roof at night.

No... It wasn't like I was waking up. It was more as if I'd been distracted and had just now noticed where I was.

The roof didn't belong to a building, a hotel, or any place on my university campus. It was the roof of my high school, and once I figured that out, I knew this was a dream.

I had no reason to sneak into the old school building. Either my high school days were still hanging around in the back of my mind and had made a random appearance in my dreams, or else...

"It's been a long time, my dear partner."

Suddenly, I sensed someone beside me. She was sitting, hugging her knees the way I was, but the gesture seemed strange coming from someone wearing a military uniform. I knew this girl's name.

"Hel."

Her red eyes smiled at me in a familiar, bewitching way.

"Did you call me here?"

Hel, who'd been Nagisa Natsunagi's alternate personality, had also been a SPES executive. At the end of our final battle with Seed, she'd vanished. Did this mean she was still watching over us somewhere?

"You're having a very convenient dream," Hel said, without answering my question. Her eyes left me, facing forward.

A convenient dream. So this was just a regular dream of talking with Hel on the roof at night, courtesy of my subconscious?

"Come to think of it, I was playing the King Game with Saikawa and the others a minute ago. I'd just become the king, and I was about to have Saikawa wear a maid outfit and call me 'Master.' Hurry up and send me back to reality."

"Never say anything that dumb in your sleep again. You know, it's been a week since you hung out with Yui Saikawa or Charlotte, and even if you did play the King Game, it's your fate to be humiliated your entire life."

Reality was way too unfair to me. Well, if that was how it was going to be, I'd soak in this dream Hel was showing me a while longer. "So how've you been, Hel? ...I guess that's a weird thing to ask, huh?"

"A bit. I've never had a physical body. I can't truly live or die. Maybe that's why I can still talk with you like this, Kimi." Hel stood up. "You seem to be doing extremely well and having a lot of fun, though."

"Do I?"

"Yes. You're with your two beloved detectives."

Describing them as "beloved" was uncalled for, but I couldn't deny that my days were pretty enjoyable. Noches had picked up on that as well.

"You can be proud of that. It's happiness you brought about, something you won. Just a few years ago, you were up on this roof lamenting the unfairness of the world."

"You mean the time I spent here with Nagisa?"

"That's right. The night when my master remembered her origins. It caused her great pain."

Yeah, the stars had been pretty then, too. Right after Nagisa had remembered who she really was and the crimes she'd committed, I'd sat here with her as she sobbed, out in the night wind.

I'd sworn to carry half the unfairness she bore, almost two years ago. But the Nagisa who'd cried back then didn't exist anymore.

"—Really?" A sudden gust of wind blew, making Hel's military uniform flutter wildly. "My master wasn't the only one. Are there really no crying girls anywhere in the world anymore?"

Hel's red eyes gazed at me, her word-soul ability forcing me to think.

A little under two decades of memories began to flow through my mind, as if my life were flashing before my eyes.

I had a nasty knack for attracting trouble. I'd seen enough heartrending tragedies to fill more than a couple of books, but the disasters had ceased a year ago. People's lives were peaceful and ordinary again. They must be. And so—

"Since we've met like this, I want you to promise me something," Hel said, without waiting for my answer.

"'Don't make Nagisa cry,' right?"

I'd made that promise to Hel before, and she'd said that if I broke it, she'd kill me enough for two—or, more concisely, double-kill me.

"Yes. You're an adult now, though, so I think I'll ask you to grow up even more and take it further." Hel had been gazing at the distant stars, but now she turned back, wearing a peaceful smile. "Don't make either of them cry—Nagisa Natsunagi, or the friend she holds dear."

The friend Nagisa held dear? Who could that be? Several faces came to mind.

I tried to respond, but then…

"—Kimihiko. Hey, Kimihiko."

Somebody called my name, and I awoke with a start.

"You were having a bad dream. Are you okay?"

A girl with red eyes and black hair was watching me worriedly. Her long hair hung down near my face, and I absently caught a few strands of it between my fingertips. "Your hair's grown."

"As compared to when? Are you still asleep?"

She really did look just like that other girl, though.

Instead of answering, I asked, "What time is it?" I'd slept a little too long; I rolled my shoulders and neck to loosen them up.

"And hey, people, don't play cards with me in the middle," I scolded. The detectives were sitting on either side of me, and their playing cards were scattered across my tray table.

We were ten thousand meters up, in a passenger plane bound for France. I glanced at my watch; about two hours had passed since takeoff.

"It's a trip, and you're sleeping right through it, Kimihiko. That's weirder."

"I agree. Assistant, the true pleasure of a trip starts while you're in transit. You're not appreciating that."

For some reason, both Nagisa and Siesta got mad at me instead. You're kidding. I'm the bad guy here?

"You two haven't changed. You're as laid-back as ever, in a good way."

Even if we were headed into danger, they were determined not to let the fun that was right in front of them go to waste. It had been like that both when I was traveling with Siesta, and when it was just Nagisa and me. They enjoyed every moment with everything they had.

"Of course, if it comes down to it, I'll switch gears immediately. Especially considering what we're dealing with this time," Siesta reassured me.

We were on our way to attend the Ritual of Sacred Return, which was scheduled for tomorrow. However, according to Noel and her people, the unknown crisis would be waiting for us there, too.

Last week, Charlie had been particularly uneasy. She'd said that if I really tried to talk them out of it, Siesta and Nagisa would probably rethink their participation. I'd ended up ignoring her advice, though, and now here we were, on the plane. And there was one major reason for that.

"Now that we know Bruno's in danger, we can't just let the situation play out," Nagisa murmured.

A few days ago, an anonymous letter had arrived at the Shirogane Detective Agency.

It had said, *The world's wisdom is about to perish.*

We didn't know whether it was a warning from the messenger from Another Eden, or from someone else entirely. But either way…

"Something's going to happen to Bruno at this ceremony, but we'll head it off. After all, we're detectives," Siesta said.

Over the past week, we'd done as much as we could. We'd imagined all sorts of situations and taken preventative measures. Even without a specific client, detectives were always there for the people.

"The detectives and their assistant really haven't changed," a voice said from above us, suddenly.

A woman had been standing in the aisle, listening in. Now she smiled, filling a paper cup with coffee.

"We have a hundred and twenty percent chance of running into you on planes, huh, Olivia?" I joked, accepting my wake-up drink.

Siesta and Nagisa greeted her with "It's been a long time."

Olivia wasn't just a cabin attendant. She was the servant of the Oracle,

one of the Tuners who protected the world, and we'd met several times before.

"How's Mia doing? Actually, is she coming to the ceremony?"

The Oracle was a former shut-in, and I hadn't seen her lately. That said, Siesta gamed with her online quite a lot, and I'd heard Mia over their voice chat every so often.

"Yes, my mistress is looking forward to seeing the three of you. Just the other day, she was busy picking out a new dress so she could wear it when you met."

"She did what?! Can she get any cuter?" Nagisa was smiling.

Mia would be nineteen this year. I couldn't wait to see her all grown up.

"Is she there already?" Siesta asked. I'd heard that Mia was still living in that clock tower in London, but…

"Madam Mia is currently carrying out her duties alone, in a certain country in northern Europe."

"She went alone…?" I asked, in spite of myself. Knowing just how reluctant Mia had been to venture into the outside world, this change surprised me. And besides… "What duties? She doesn't have that ability anymore, does she?"

"That's right. At present, Madam Mia no longer prophesies global crises. However, she still worries about the world. She takes frequent journeys so that she can see what's happening with her own eyes. Just as you once did," Olivia said, gazing at us kindly. "In addition, something that will require us to act may happen soon."

…Oh, so Olivia and Mia knew the unknown crisis might occur at the ceremony, too? That was why Mia was still doing everything she could, even without her power.

"If Mia's traveling, does that mean you're here for your regular job today?"

"Yes, I'm performing my duties as cabin attendant as well, but…" Taking an attaché case from the service cart, Olivia showed us its contents. "Here. The origin text."

The impossible appearance of this rare item made me freeze up. This was what Noel had told us about: the volume scheduled to make its first appearance at the Ritual of Sacred Return. The most important one. Why was it here?

"The Oracle instructed me to give this to you, Mr. Kimizuka, no matter what rules were broken in the process."

"...To me? I don't get it. Does she want me to deliver it or something? That can't be right."

If Mia was going to attend the ceremony herself, she should have brought it with her, or at least had her servant Olivia handle it. Plus, Mia was the only one who was allowed to read the sacred texts at all. That had to be even more true of the origin text.

"Even so, the Oracle has entrusted this to you. As for what she meant by it..."

Olivia handed the origin text to me.

"I believe that may be up to you, as '——.'"

A vibration ran through the plane, drowning out the noise around us.

Had we hit some major turbulence? For a moment, I felt as if I'd passed out. The next thing I knew, I was gripping the origin text tightly.

"...! Olivia, are you okay?" I asked. My mouth had gone dry.

"...? Yes. Never mind me, you're the one who's..." Olivia was gazing at me curiously.

"Seriously, Kimihiko, what's the matter? You're sweating like crazy." Nagisa was also watching me, looking puzzled.

I wiped my forehead. How was I sweating this much after such a brief moment? "...Yeah, I'm fine. Never mind that, what time is it?"

"Huh? Didn't you just ask me that?"

I looked at the watch on my left wrist. It had only been a little over two hours since takeoff. The coffee sitting on the tray table was still hot.

"Assistant?"

When I tried to look out the window, I made eye contact with the other detective. Siesta was staring at me; she seemed mystified and just a little uneasy. "I'm fine," I said again.

"That's what people say when they aren't fine."

"The way the plane shook back there scared me, that's all. I'll calm down if you hold my hand or something."

"Are you stupid, Kimi?"

"Man, that's not fair."

It seemed like it had been a while since we'd had one of these exchanges. Maybe it was because there were fewer opportunities to feel the world was unfair these days—so maybe it wasn't such a bad thing. Actually, wasn't it better not to have people calling me stupid? I was getting all mixed up.

"Sorry. I really am fine now."

That dumb little mental tangent had helped me to relax a bit.

While I was reassuring Siesta, I stowed the origin text in my carry-on bag.

After another ten-plus hours of flight time, we reached our destination.

Then we waited to pick up our checked suitcases…but for some reason, mine never showed up.

By the time I'd finally recovered my luggage, bemoaning my talent for inconvenient incidents, Nagisa and Siesta were already gone. They'd given up on me and headed for our hotel pretty fast.

"Why are they both so mean? At least one of them should be nice."

As I was walking through the airport, grumbling to myself, I spotted a tall man talking to a young girl. He was speaking French, and I couldn't catch a lot of it, but he kept pointing to the camera he was holding. Was he telling the girl he wanted a photo?

"Well, I get why he'd want her to model for him."

The gray-haired girl had a cool, expressionless face, and she was wearing a particularly eye-catching Gothic Lolita dress. She was my friend… Well, maybe I wouldn't go that far, but anyway, she was definitely Noel de Lupwise.

Had she come to the airport to meet us? I decided to lend her a hand and headed over toward them. I thought about going full TV drama and saying, "What do you want with my girl?" but I wasn't sure I really wanted to do that.

Come to think of it, I remembered Noel mentioning something about how she wished I'd been part of her family. In that case…

"Oh!" Noel had spotted me.

Stepping in front of her, I faced the man with the camera and said, in clumsy French...

"What do you want with my little sister?"

◆ "Elder Brother" is tempting, too

"Thanks for the ride," I told Noel, climbing into the waiting car.

The interior of the shiny black luxury car was roomy enough for me to stretch my legs out. They even had champagne back there, although since it was only ten minutes from here to the hotel, it wasn't like we'd have time for a drink... Or so I thought, but Noel held out a glass to me and said, "Please have some." *I guess I'll do that, then.*

"Of course I'd come to pick you up. You're an important guest."

Noel was as doll-like as ever, and her expression never changed much, but she was smiling gently. I wished the other government officials would take a page from her book. Siesta and Nagisa too, actually. They'd just straight-up left me.

"Besides, I'm the one who's grateful. Thank you very much for rescuing me—Brother."

I spit out my champagne.

"Oh! Are you all right? I'm sorry. Did it not suit your preferences? Driver, take us to a vineyard at once—"

"It's fine; just head for the hotel. You don't have to harvest grapes or let them age or anything." I mopped up the spilled champagne with my handkerchief. "Did you call me your brother, Noel?"

"Um, did I say something strange?"

Basically everything you said was strange, yeah.

I regretted impulsively running my mouth at the airport now. What scared me the most was that she might call me that in front of Siesta or Nagisa.

"I seem to have offended you. I'm very sorry." Noel bowed her head respectfully. "Would this do, then?" She gazed into my eyes. "Bro."

"Ngh." I had a heart attack and collapsed.

"Are you stupid, Kimi?"

Even Siesta was showing up in my head. I was terminal.

"Heh-heh. I'm sorry. That was a little sister joke. Forgive me, please." Noel did her best to keep her usual serious expression from slipping, but from time to time, she kicked her feet a little. She might not have known she was doing it.

"Now then, Mr. Kimihiko."

"You're going back to calling me that already?"

"Could we speak about that other matter for just a moment?"

Apparently, we were done joking around. When I heard the phrase "that other matter," only one thing came to mind. "You mean Bruno?"

That mystery letter which had been sent to our agency a few days earlier: *The world's wisdom is about to perish.* We'd promptly shared that information with Noel, but we hadn't discussed it in detail yet.

"The thing is, we know almost nothing about it, either. We haven't looked into it enough yet."

"...I see. No, there's no helping that. It isn't technically a job for the Ace Detectives."

Siesta and Nagisa's initial orders had only been to get through the unknown crisis and make sure the Ritual of Sacred Return was completed. This business with Bruno was a curveball.

"If Bruno really is in danger at the ceremony, though, our detectives won't just stand by. They won't care about the specifics of their roles or missions." We'd just talked about their resolve in the plane on the way here. "What about you, Noel? Do you have any suggestions for ways to protect Bruno?"

"Yes. Frankly, I think it would be safest to cancel the Ritual of Sacred Return entirely... But practically speaking, that would be difficult. The Federation Government wants to host the ritual, burn the origin text, and bring about world peace as soon as possible."

Noel had told us as much the first time we'd met her: They planned to put a permanent end to the world's disasters by burning the origin text and returning the Oracle's power to the gods.

"It's really true? If we complete the Ritual of Sacred Return, global crises will never happen again?"

That might be something Mia, who possessed the origin text, would understand instinctively. As someone who wasn't directly involved, though, I could only take that statement as hearsay.

"...Yes, there's no mistake." Noel's eyes wavered slightly. "It's corroborated by several millennia of records. If the Ritual of Sacred Return is completed, you and the detectives will never be dragged into global crises again."

When I heard Noel's words, I had the feeling I knew why she had hesitated.

If it was "corroborated by several millennia of records," the Ritual of Sacred Return had been held before. If they were trying to hold it again anyway, that probably meant... No, that wasn't important now. She'd told me what I wanted to know. For now, I just said, "I see," and went on. "Could we just have Bruno stay home, then?"

People were attending the ritual by invitation, so he had to have the right to decline.

"I really would have preferred that. However..."

I knew where that sentence was going. Bruno must have refused.

An understandable choice, given his position. He was the one who'd asked Siesta and Nagisa to fight the unknown crisis, so the danger to himself must not have been enough of a reason for him to leave the battlefield.

"It would help a lot if the enemy's demands were a bit easier to understand, at least." We would have had room to negotiate or put together a strategy, then. However, the messengers from Another Eden wanted something specific from the Federation Government, but we didn't know what that thing was.

"...As a matter of fact, I've heard a rumor about that."

"Really?"

"Yes. They say the officials of the Federation Government once hid *a certain important secret* in Pandora's box. At this point, no one knows what it is... However, the messengers of Another Eden may have managed to find out."

Noel told me it was a rumor she'd first heard only after she became a government official. The enemy had learned about an important secret the

Federation Government had kept hidden for ages, and was threatening them.

"What should I do? How can I protect both the world and Grandfather?" Noel murmured. There was something almost self-deprecating about the way she said it.

That worry was based in her complicated position. First and foremost, as a Federation Government official, she needed to have Bruno—a former Tuner—fight the unknown crisis. After all, that was the system of justice they'd built for this world.

However, Noel had another relationship with Bruno. He was family. If she treasured that relationship, of course she'd want him to stay away from the ceremony.

"Bruno's presence in your life is just that big, huh?"

"...Yes. Grandfather was my only ally, and my only family."

Then, quietly, Noel began to tell me about herself. Fifteen years ago, she'd been born into the Lupwise family, which was of French nobility, with ties to the Federation Government. However, the head of the family had fathered her with one of the maids. Noel's mother was promptly run out of the mansion, and both her father and his legal wife had distanced themselves from Noel's birth.

"The Lupwise family always treated me as someone who didn't exist. No one spoke to me or answered my questions. Not my grandparents, or my parents, or my older brother, or even the servants. In that house, I was invisible."

"And Bruno saved you from that?"

Noel gazed out the car window. "Yes," she said, smiling very slightly. "One day ten years ago, Grandfather rescued me from that house. I'd never spoken with anyone before, but he gave me language, and taught me how to smile and how to get angry. I was invisible, but he made me human again."

Noel and Bruno's relationship wasn't something I could make sense of on my own. There was a decade-long bond between them that only they could understand, just like the one I had with the detectives.

"However, I've been on my own again for the past year."

Noel's voice was low, but it reached me without being drowned out by the noise of the traffic.

Three years ago, Noel had begun to work as a Federation Government official in place of her older brother, who'd disappeared. Last year, Bruno had formally dissolved their relationship, and she had left the Belmondo family entirely.

"I'm sure the real reason he schedules dinners for the two of us every once in a while is that... Hm?"

Noel's cheeks deflated, and her lips got narrower—because I was pinching her cheek.

"He taught you how to smile, didn't he? You're supposed to do what your parents taught you."

"Mrph," Noel said.

I pushed the corner of her mouth up. "Let's try talking to Bruno one more time." When I let go, Noel stared at me, surprised. "There may still be something we can do. Some way to protect both the world and Bruno. We'll think about it together a little more."

Right now, Noel couldn't afford to lose Bruno.

As she wavered between her mission and self-interest, she seemed like a mirror reflecting a certain someone else.

◆ Mission Start

Soon after that, the car reached our destination.

I parted from Noel, walked into the hotel she'd reserved for us, and took the elevator up.

It was a luxury resort hotel, the kind we'd never have been able to stay at as a rule. When I knocked on the door of a room on the thirty-fifth floor, Siesta opened it. "Oh, you're finally here."

"...You're a heartless fiend."

"I am not. I just believed that no matter what trouble you got into, you were bound to come out victorious, so I went on ahead to the hotel."

Geez. It's all in how you phrase things, isn't it?

I went inside, dragging my suitcase. Our room turned out to be a suite, with a living room that was separate from the bedroom. The detectives had been having their afternoon tea in there: Snacks and a teapot were set out on the table.

"Huh? Are you staying here, too, Kimihiko?"

When she saw me wearily grab a chair and sit down, Nagisa blinked at me.

"Yeah. I told Noel it was fine to put us all in the same room."

"Gosh, I feel threatened."

"Don't squirm when you say that."

"I didn't!"

As we were having that fun conversation, Siesta brought me a cup. "You're having tea, too, aren't you, Kimi?"

"Oh… Nah, water's fine." I picked up a plastic bottle of mineral water that was already sitting there.

"…I see." For some reason, Siesta looked a little disappointed. She sat down next to me. "Kimi, have you been drinking? You smell like liquor."

"I just had a glass in the car on the way here. Noel offered."

"And you always tell me not to drink."

That's her own fault. After all, drinking has helped this detective blow it before.

"Wait, you saw Noel? Does that mean you talked about the Bruno thing?" Nagisa asked, tossing a chocolate into her mouth.

"Yeah. She said he's still planning to go to the ceremony."

"…I see. Then we really will have to make thorough preparations before the Ritual of Sacred Return."

"That's probably the whole reason Noel came to us about this. It sounds like they haven't been able to contact most of the other Tuners."

As Siesta said, at this point, the Ace Detective was the only former Tuner who specialized in combat. And even that was only true of Siesta, not Nagisa.

"Hm? What?" Siesta noticed my gaze and tilted her head.

"I just sort of wished we at least had Charlie here."

"She's on a different mission right now."

A week ago, Charlie had been on the fence about attending the Ritual of Sacred Return, and she'd ultimately decided not to come. Her reasons hadn't been pessimistic, though: The agent had picked up another important mission.

"What's she up to now? Even you don't know, do you, Siesta?"

"Right, but that's how it should be with Charlie," Siesta said, gazing into the distance. I sensed a little pride in her profile.

Exactly. Charlotte wasn't just an agent who tagged along after the detective anymore.

"I wonder if Yui's running around getting ready for her overseas performance," Nagisa murmured, checking her phone. Come to think of it, the concert was the day after tomorrow.

"By the way, I just sent her a text asking 'What are you doing now?', and she replied with 'Please don't act like you're my boyfriend.'"

"Geez, Yui. Ouch."

After we'd talked about that for a while...

"So, Siesta. What are we going to do now? Either way, I think we should talk to Bruno a bit more."

"At this stage, we should probably set up safeguards to minimize the damage in case there really is an attack during the Ritual of Sacred Return." Gazing at her smartphone, Siesta started to go over our course of action.

"Huh? Wait, we haven't filled our assistant in on this maneuver yet, have we?"

"I have one other piece of insurance. Or maybe I should say I'm working on something, but...I guess it doesn't have to be now."

"Hey, you two. Quit messing around with your phones and let me in on this."

Granted, there had been one very recent incident where everything had worked out much better because the whole team wasn't on the same page, but...

"Well, if it comes to that, I've got an ace up my sleeve, too."

"Oh, yay. I'm happy for you."

Siesta, it actually hurts kind of a lot when you dodge the subject like that.

"But listen, we may need to designate someone to call the shots," Nagisa said.

True—no matter how we strategized and planned, it would be pointless if we couldn't make prompt decisions when it counted.

"Why not our assistant?" Siesta suggested unexpectedly.

Both Nagisa and I weren't sure what she was getting at.

"Nagisa, you and I were the ones who decided to reclaim our authority as Tuners, attend the Ritual of Sacred Return, and take on the unknown crisis. That means it's Kimi's turn. We'll let him have the right to make the final decisions and give the orders," Siesta said, poking my cheek with her fingertip several times.

"This is proof that you trust me, right?" I said. "You're not just shoving all the responsibility onto me, are you?"

As I tried to smile, several texts came in on my phone.

"...Oh, I see."

For a brief moment, I made eye contact with each detective.

The mission was already underway.

◆ Eden's messenger

When the sun had descended another thirty degrees...

"How pretty! It's like we're in a movie!"

From the little boat that was sailing down the river, the townscape seemed to be dissolving into the sunset. Drinking in the view, Nagisa gave a blissful sigh. After relaxing in our hotel room for a bit, the detectives and I had decided to see the sights of Paris on a cruise down the Seine.

The excursion wouldn't quite take an hour, and we'd be able to see the Eiffel Tower and the Pont Alexandre III from the water. However, due to a certain situation, the tour was due to be discontinued soon, and we'd just barely gotten to enjoy this cinematic scenery.

"I've been through so much that could have been straight out of a movie—I'm sort of sick of it," Siesta mused. She stood on the deck with us, a wine glass full of juice in one hand. As she'd said, we'd starred in all sorts of movies, from spy-action flicks to science fiction B movies, and of course detective films.

"The only genre that never showed up was romance."

"True. That might have been the leading actor's fault, though."

Both Nagisa and Siesta gave me significant looks.

"Not fair." That seemed the best moment to lodge a complaint as I drank my wine. Its astringent taste made my mouth sting a bit; like coffee, the flavor had a surprising depth to it.

"You're all quite grown-up, aren't you?" Noel murmured, gazing at us. She was the one who'd arranged this exclusive tour. "It's clear that you've experienced many things I couldn't even imagine, gotten through them, and formed a special relationship only the three of you can understand."

The three of us looked at each other. We were all wearing different expressions. Siesta's was prim, but there was pride there as well. Although Nagisa appeared satisfied, her smile wasn't entirely joyful... I wondered what my face looked like to them.

"I wonder what your relationship would be called in Japanese. I don't think it's a 'three-way standoff'... Oh! A 'love triangle.'"

"Let's get down to business." Blocking out the ominous phrase Noel had just dropped, I turned to look at the other individual who was present. "You really won't excuse yourself from tomorrow's ceremony, Bruno?"

The old gentleman was standing a little apart from our group, wine glass in hand, gazing out over the river. Noel had called him here as well.

"Yes. You know I mustn't make you stand on the battlefield while I sit reading in the shade." As we'd heard earlier, Bruno meant to prioritize his own mission. "If I yield to the enemy now, I'll disgrace the name of justice. I will not submit to any threat."

"Grandfather..." Noel gave Bruno a concerned look.

"There's no need to worry. Besides, if the messenger from Another Eden is targeting the Federation Government, then even you are in danger, Noel. Isn't that right?"

"Yes, but...the enemy has singled you out by name, Grandfather. I think you should be extremely cautious, and that finding out why they did that is an urgent matter."

Bruno and Noel's worry for each other was putting them in conflict, but no compromise presented itself.

"I think Noel has a point, though." Nagisa broke into their conversation. "Why would the messenger from Another Eden be after Bruno in particular? He isn't the only one who's working with the Federation Government."

She was right. If they were after people who were working with the government and trying to shut down the unknown crisis, the two detectives fit the description as well.

"In the first place, I really doubt your letter was sent by Another Eden's messenger," Bruno said, overturning our premise. "I hear they've never tried to contact the Federation Government by mail. Am I right, Noel?"

"...Yes. In simple terms, they use 'signals'—in the electrical engineering sense—to send their messages to electronic terminals in a language we can understand. But no matter how we try, we haven't been able to analyze that program."

This was giving me a headache, but basically, they couldn't trace the source of Another Eden's transmissions through their logs. Come to think of it, I'd heard something about that earlier... At any rate, the residents of Another Eden had some seriously unfamiliar technology.

"Then the letter was sent by someone completely different." Siesta might have assumed there was a good chance of that all along; she nodded, seeming convinced.

"Yes. However, it doesn't matter who is targeting me. Even after the Great Cataclysm, I haven't let my guard down in the slightest. The light of justice has never been extinguished. No matter what enormous evil presents itself, I'll intercept it," Bruno said, gazing out at the majestic river. Several wild birds flew across the water.

"It looks like rain," Siesta said casually, without even glancing at the sky.

"Rain? The clouds don't look that thick."

"Did you see how close those birds were to the river's surface? They were after the bugs; humidity weighs insects down."

Siesta's instincts were based in analysis, and they were usually right. If it was going to rain, it might be a good idea to finish the tour early.

"And my old wound is hurting a little." Siesta pressed a hand to the left side of her chest.

Right after I'd focused on her gesture, it happened.

Something else arrived before the rain did.

"—Why can you not comprehend our demand?"

The source of the voice was several meters above our heads, on the boat's mast. Even though there was practically nothing to use as a foothold, a figure in a crow mask and a red robe was standing up there.

"Kimihiko, that's…"

"…Yeah. Let's back up."

Realizing more or less what this was, Nagisa and I backed away.

"Federation Government Tuners Respond."

The thing twisted its head ninety degrees. Its voice sounded mechanical, but it was capable of communicating verbally.

"Who are you?" Siesta raised her musket. She wasn't shaken or anxious. She meant to carry out her role, just as she'd always done. However, Bruno gently held up a hand in front of her, telling her to stand down.

"Are you the messenger from Another Eden?" he asked the masked figure, as calmly as he could.

"There is no meaning in your name for us." That sounded like a "yes." And then… **"We only want the world's secret."**

This messenger from an unknown world was attempting to negotiate with us in a language we'd understand. "The world's secret" had to be what they were demanding from the Federation Government. However…

"You aren't giving us enough information." Noel took a step forward. "The Federation Government isn't rejecting you outright. We simply don't know what you mean by 'the world's secret.' That leaves us with no way to negotiate."

"Why?" The crow-mask bent its neck in the opposite direction. **"Why don't you comprehend? Why did you forget?"**

The next instant, an unpleasant sound like broken-up static ran through my inner ears. My hands came up to cover them, and I squeezed my eyes shut. When I opened them again, the surface of the water around the boat was littered with dead fish and birds.

"Noel, get back." Siesta stepped in front of her, pointing her musket at the thing in the crow mask. "What do you mean, 'we forgot'? Maybe we never knew."

"Just try and shoot."

Siesta scowled, but she pulled the trigger. The bullet moved too fast to be seen, but just before it reached its target, it stopped—and abruptly disappeared. It was as if it had been sucked through a dimensional crack.

"Negotiations are canceled."

With that mechanical declaration, the denizen of Eden turned to go.

"Wait," Siesta said sharply.

The next thing I knew, a few scattered drops of rain had begun to fall.

"Tell your companions that, as things stand, your request will not be granted. Tell them to consider their own goals first, then tell us what they are."

She wasn't holding her gun at the ready anymore.

However, the detective's words were more relentless and passionate than any weapon. "We aren't currently fighting in the same ring, and we haven't arrived at the same negotiation table. If you still try to hurt this world or my companions, I'll ignore the rule of nonaggression. I will march into Eden or hell, and I will fight. I swear it."

The crow mask's big, black, hollow eyes were fixed on Siesta. However, no words issued from its large beak.

◆ The ignorant king

There was a certain custom that the detectives and I had followed for ages: When we resolved an incident, we'd reward ourselves with afternoon tea or a good dinner. We'd discuss the case, reflect on any errors, and learn what we could from it.

Now that we were a bit older, the form of that ritual had changed slightly. Sometimes we had wine or cocktails after our meal instead of tea or coffee. Either way, it was an important part of our work communication, and so we'd gone to a pub, but…

"Haaah. What did that thing in the crow mask want, anyway?" Nagisa sighed, setting down her mug of beer.

Two hours ago, the messenger from Another Eden had appeared on that small boat, then left just as abruptly. Since there was nothing we could do about it, our group had split up. Then, even though we hadn't resolved the incident, Nagisa, Siesta, and I had come to this bar in the hopes of venting some of our frustration. And Nagisa and I weren't the only ones drinking…

"Some people say melons are vegetables, but I think they're fruits, you know. A long time ago, a famous comedian said that if something goes well with mayonnaise, it's a vegetable, and if it doesn't, it's a fruit. So I tried putting mayonnaise on melon, and it was absolutely delish, so guess what? Melons are actually vegetables."

The white-haired detective was babbling incoherently over a glass of red wine. Her skin was flushed, and her eyes were glazed. As I'd anticipated, she was a little more wound-up than usual.

This was how Siesta usually got when she drank, so I'd banned her from having alcohol…but Nagisa and I had looked away for a second, Siesta had gotten some wine into her system, and now here we were.

"Heyyy, Assistant. Are you listening?" Siesta pouted, trying to pick a fight with me.

"Yeah, you were listing your favorite fruits. Hurry up and tell me your top three." Casually fielding the drunk detective, I sipped water. If I drank too much myself, I might do something stupid.

"…Somebody's not really into this conversation. What, drinking with me isn't fun for you?" Siesta glared at me. "You've seemed bored this whole time. You're barely reacting to anything I say."

Yeesh. When Siesta had gotten drunk before, even brushing her off like that would have put a cheerful smile on her face. She must've built up a tolerance. I hadn't thought I was being that openly critical of her behavior, but she'd picked up on it anyway.

"About what happened on the cruise." Setting my glass down, I averted my eyes. "Why did you say that to the enemy, there at the end?"

"…Say what? I don't really remember."

If she was playing dumb, that meant she remembered it clearly.

Siesta had said she'd march into Eden and fight to protect the world or her companions, even if it meant breaking a nonaggression pact. That remark of hers was the biggest reason for the frustration that was smoldering inside me.

"The Ritual of Sacred Return is tomorrow. Once that's over, you and Nagisa won't be Tuners anymore. You won't have to deal with Another Eden."

"We don't know whether they'll manage to complete that ritual. Until we settle the unknown crisis the crow-masked messenger and its friends are plotting, I'll keep fighting. Which part of that do you have a problem with, Kimi?"

Siesta drained her mineral water. The ice in her glass clinked. Her head must have cooled down, too.

"Why do you need to be the one who does that, Siesta?"

"Because I'm the Ace Detective."

"Technically, you're still a proxy."

"I'll do it even if I'm just a detective."

"—! Why would you go that far...?"

Our exchange was brief. Neither of us was drunk anymore, but our heated emotions hadn't cooled.

"Because you two did this for me." Siesta turned her blue eyes on me, then promptly averted them again. "Long ago, you risked your lives to save me, so I'll do the same. This has nothing to do with jobs and missions. If anyone tries to hurt something that's precious to me, I'll fight with everything I have, and I'll protect both of you."

She snapped her mouth shut after that.

The pub's quiet background music and other customers' conversations filled the silence between us. It had been a long time since I'd argued with Siesta like this.

Nagisa was the one to break the silence completely. "Okay, that's enough." She clapped her hands once, sharply, softening the tension. "And while I'm at it, hiyah!"

There was a dull *thunk* as her fists connected with my head and Siesta's.

"Ow! Hey, Nagisa...!"

"...That was mean. What was that for?"

Siesta and I turned accusatory looks on her, but she didn't back down. Instead, she heaved a big sigh. "I'll double-kill you both. Well? Did that calm you down a bit?"

…If that was what she'd been trying to do, the clap at the beginning probably would've been enough. Sheesh.

"Sorry. I guess I had a little too much to drink. Blame it on the alcohol, okay?" I apologized to Nagisa.

"I'm sorry, too, Nagisa. Blame it on our assistant this time."

She was so damn mean. I glared at Siesta from under half-closed eyelids, and she snubbed me.

Nagisa sighed again. "Haaah. Geez." And then... "But I guess that's where it's at for both of you," she murmured quietly, gazing at the ceiling. "C'mon, Siesta. Let's head back to the hotel. Can you stand?" Nagisa helped Siesta up, and they turned to go.

"So you're just leaving me here?"

"If you're together, you two will just fight again, right? A little distance is a good thing sometimes. Besides," Nagisa added, "you have another job to do, right, Kimihiko?"

…Yeah, I did. It was a job Siesta had asked me to handle. In preparation, I relocated to a seat at the bar by myself. "Okay, Nagisa. Take care of Siesta."

Siesta had her back to me. I could tell she'd heard me, but she left with Nagisa without giving me another look.

"Even I've never seen Daydream like that before."

How long had he been there, watching us? The old man was sitting three seats away, drinking whiskey, wearing the same suit he'd worn earlier.

Bruno Belmondo. The person I was waiting for.

"I arrived a little early. Your lively dinner was a nice show to go with my drink." Bruno smiled. I'd stayed behind because I needed to talk with him a little more. I never thought he'd been watching us the entire time, though.

"Sorry you had to see that weird infighting."

"No, no. It was novel to see her display that sort of emotion. Still, I imagine she did it because it was an earnest exchange with someone who required honesty. I don't think it was wrong."

Bruno set his glass down on the bar. At some point, all the other customers had left the pub. The only sound was pleasant jazz playing softly in the background.

"Now then, could you tell me why you called me here? You said this talk would be confidential." Bruno drained his whiskey, then looked over at me, a few seats away.

"Yeah. Bruno, why are you so set on fighting this unknown crisis?"

This was the same thing Siesta and I had just argued about.

It might have seemed strange for me to ask him about that now. However, as the assistant, getting the answer out of him was my job.

"Why would you bring that up now? Isn't it a bit late for that?"

"I thought it might be a hard question to answer if Noel was around."

Because they were family. There are some things that are hard to say to someone precisely because you trust them. That's how it works for me, anyway.

"Because I am a Tuner. Because it's a hero's natural duty. Isn't that answer enough?"

"I'm not asking about your profile."

During a job just the other day, I'd learned you can't assume you know somebody just because you're familiar with their social status, job title, and career.

"—Long ago, I traveled."

Bruno seemed to have given in. Still facing forward, he began telling his story. "As a young reporter, I left on a rambling journey to learn about the world. In the midst of my travels, I was drawn to a certain country's culture and ended up spending many years there."

What I was hearing was the past of an extremely learned information broker who'd lived more than a century. I listened carefully.

According to Bruno, while the country was small, it had plentiful energy resources and was quite wealthy.

"Its abundance was bait for invaders, however. Before long, the neighboring military states pressed the country to sign a series of unfair treaties. The country's king accepted all the terms they set. He believed he had no choice if he wanted to protect his people."

Bruno had been against that policy, but at the time, he'd been a mere traveling journalist. He didn't have the power to make a country do anything.

"Contrary to my expectations, the country's peace was preserved. It wasn't as wealthy as it had once been, but at the very least, its people weren't ravaged by war. The king's wise decision had protected the country. I felt ashamed," Bruno murmured.

He said it had been a mistake for him to weigh the country's wealth against its citizens' lives. That king was beloved by his people, and he'd lived out his life happily until his death from old age.

"What country are we talking about?" I asked. His story had ended happily, and I was curious about what had happened after.

"It doesn't have a name," Bruno said simply. "In today's world, it no longer exists. Fifteen years after that king passed away, the country's economy collapsed. It was carved up by the alliance and vanished off the map."

Considering Bruno's age, this had happened about a hundred years ago. There probably wasn't anyone else on the planet who could give a firsthand account of what had happened. It was a true story only Bruno could tell.

"The great king died in ignorance. He passed away beloved by his people, unaware of his crime."

Bruno's eyes narrowed, as if he was faintly remembering a distant day. I didn't know what to say.

"The moral of this story isn't that we must take up our weapons and fight; only that we must search for a way to protect the world, and that our efforts must be constant."

I couldn't find the words I needed to say. Even so, I could tell that Bruno's philosophy wasn't wrong.

"If the world is approaching another turning point, we must act with purpose. At the coming Ritual of Sacred Return, we must demonstrate our determination to protect the world, even if the unknown crisis is an attempt to get in our way."

This was Bruno Belmondo's resolution: a great will which had nothing to do with his title or profile, formed by the history he'd lived through.

"Therefore, boy, I would like you to pay more attention to Noel than to me. Protect the young person who has a future rather than an old life that's nearing its end, won't you?"

I wasn't a detective, but I was human, and that meant I had to grant Bruno's request. Except...

"What if I save both of you? Won't that work?"

I knew it was an arrogant suggestion, but I made it anyway. That was what my partners would have said if they were here, I think.

"You're right. The Ritual of Sacred Return should take place. The detectives and I will guarantee that it does, so would you let us handle things tomorrow and spend the day somewhere safe instead?" I took a certain object out of my bag. "This is the origin text, and I swear to take it to the ceremony."

"...I see. Did the young Oracle entrust it to you?"

Mia Whitlock, the Oracle who saw all futures, had handed me the reins of tomorrow's fate.

"The Oracle has already lost her power, though. There is no one in the world who can truly predict the future." Bruno shook his head, refusing to change his answer. "Can you bring about the tomorrow you wish for in the midst of such uncertainty?"

"But instead of the future, you know everything about the world, right?" I pointed out.

Silence fell for a moment... But only a moment.

"Yes, that's true. I know. I know everything. However, I merely know it. I can't necessarily deduce the right answer. I may even give a wrong one."

That was Bruno's calm analysis of his own position and abilities. He said that simply knowing, simply having all the data, didn't guarantee that people could come up with the right answer on their own.

In my case—I'd always had someone who could show me whether I was right in those moments. If I went way back in time, the man who'd called himself my teacher had been that person. Then it had been Siesta. After she was gone, Nagisa had come along. Now I had lots of friends who would help me search for answers.

But Bruno was supposed to be all-knowing. What if he got an answer wrong? If that day came, what then?

"If I give a wrong answer someday, no doubt someone will appear to correct it. That is how the world is kept in tune." Bruno drained the last of his whiskey.

"You really think someone who can correct the world's wisdom will come along?"

"Yes. What do you suppose a person like that would be called?"

I didn't have a clever answer for that question.

With a merry laugh, Bruno got to his feet. "Ha-ha. There's no way I'd know. After all, such a person would be beyond me."

Then, walking with the aid of his cane, Bruno left by himself.

Liquor made us human again.

Both the detective and the sage, the maiden and the old man. Everyone, equally.

When everyone was gone, I stood up to leave, too. Just then, my phone, which was resting on the bar, lit up. It was a notification from my messaging app. I had a text from Nagisa.

"When you get back, want to talk for a bit?"

Just as I picked up my phone to respond, a call came in from a withheld number.

"Coincidences never happen alone, huh?"

Should I respond to Nagisa's text or take the call?

I hesitated, and then I—

◆ Even if justice dies

When I got out of the car that had come for me, I found myself at a temple, or maybe the site of a ruin.

Bright moonlight streamed into the roofless building, and vines coiled around the structure here and there. Parts of the walls and pillars had crumbled, but I could still tell that this place had once been majestic.

The rain that had been falling since the evening had stopped at some point.

In addition to the moonlight, minimal lighting had been installed on the ground, providing visibility even at night. As a result, I saw the person who'd summoned me here quite clearly.

"It's been a long time, Stephen."

The man was wearing his familiar white lab coat, and he was standing with his back to me. His hands were busy with something. "I'm sorry to ask this of you after calling you here, but wait just a few minutes," he said. The screen of the small monitor in front of him showed a pulsing red organ—a throbbing heart. Then a hand holding a scalpel appeared on the screen, but that hand wasn't human. It was a robotic arm.

"Remote surgery?"

The technology had become practical several years ago. At this point, it was possible for surgeons to perform operations from a different location by using a robot proxy.

However, I'd heard that only a handful of doctors could conduct remote operations that required high-level skill and precision, such as heart surgery and live-donor liver transplants. They would have to be virtuoso doctors like Stephen Bluefield, the former Inventor.

"They told me you were missing."

I'd never dreamed I'd meet him here, of all places.

"As long as people live, there will always be work for doctors. Even now, people are screaming for help to save fading lives in the hidden corners of the world," Stephen said, without looking back.

Surgery performed by moonlight. On the screen, the robotic arm followed the movements of his fingertips perfectly.

"In many areas of the world, there are still land mines that were buried in wartime. Remote surgery is also useful in regions that aren't easily accessed."

Maybe there were no more global crises, but it wasn't as if war had disappeared entirely, and the aftermath of past disasters hadn't been completely cleared away.

Even now that Stephen was no longer the Inventor, he was still working as a doctor. It was similar to the way Siesta had continued working as a private eye, even though she wasn't the Ace Detective anymore.

"Thank you for waiting."

Then Stephen powered down the monitor and turned to face me.

The whole process struck me as remarkably fast, but apparently he'd just performed the steps only he was capable of, and doctors who were physically on-site were taking care of the rest. This was more efficient and let him help the maximum number of patients. He'd told me about his philosophy as a doctor before.

"Thanks to you, both Nagisa and Siesta are doing great. Once again, I'm grateful."

It had been about a year since I'd last spoken with Stephen.

The former Inventor had saved the lives of both detectives multiple times, and a year ago, he'd had a hand in the event that had awakened Siesta.

"No, I haven't done a thing," Stephen said, gazing up at the night sky. He wasn't trying to be modest.

"So, Stephen. Is what you told me true?"

At the bar where I'd talked with Bruno, I'd gotten a phone call. When I'd followed the instructions I was given and climbed into the car he'd sent for me, I'd ended up here.

"If there really is a way to prevent the unknown crisis, then tell me about it."

I hadn't believed him right away. I'd decided to accept his invitation because if I didn't hear him out, there'd be things I wouldn't know.

"It's true. We've been searching for a method the entire time."

We? Was there somebody else here? As I looked around, the room was flooded with bright light from the floor. Those shafts of light illuminated an enormous object that towered behind Stephen.

"A gun turret?"

The thing was like a monument, so tall I had to tilt my head back to see it. Now that I was paying attention, I saw that it was covered in vines. The iron cylinder towering into the sky really did look like a cannon.

"This is an ancient relic. It isn't used anymore," Stephen told me. His eyes were on the object, too. "Where do you suppose the muzzle is pointing?"

In the next moment, I realized there were two silhouettes near the weapon. No, not just near it: One of them was actually sitting cross-legged on top of the enormous gun.

"That's…"

The man was wearing a biker jacket and a robotic-looking mask that covered his whole head. His face, which was turned toward us, was blinking with a weird green light. I knew that guy. I'd first seen him ten years ago—in a certain movie that had been shown all across the US and become an instant blockbuster.

Full-Face, a former Tuner. His position was Hero.

In the *Full-Face* action movie series, a man who wore a motorcycle helmet developed superhuman powers one day and fought an evil organization. Surprisingly, the starring actor was a hero in the real world as well. Just like in the movie, he used actual superhuman powers, and he'd defeated all sorts of dangerous enemies with his own hands.

The other individual, who was standing near Stephen, was a tall, veiled woman in a dress with slits up the sides. Even though I couldn't see her face, I could feel her aura as if it were an electrical current.

She was the former Tuner Youkaki. Her position had been Revolutionary.

She was so stunning that her beauty alone was said to be a weapon that could bring down nations. She'd inherited her position after the death of Fritz Stewart, the previous Revolutionary. How many countries had been destroyed as a result of her covert maneuvering? Although her peerless beauty was renowned, her face was always veiled, and regular people never got the chance to see it.

"Stephen, are you telling me the three of you have been searching for a way to prevent the unknown crisis?" I asked. It was hard to believe. Both Full-Face and Youkaki preferred to work alone, and it was rare for them to show themselves like this. Besides...

"If you've gotten this many former Tuners together, Bruno must have contacted you as well. Didn't he ask you to prevent the unknown crisis with him?"

"Yes, but I turned him down," Stephen said bluntly. "The Information Broker has his eyes on the same goal as us, but he's far too unwilling to compromise. If it's for the sake of justice, he's prepared to return his body to the dust this very moment. And I think that's dangerous." He turned to me. "Kimihiko Kimizuka. I believe we feel the same way, correct?"

I wanted to deny it.

He'd seen right through me, though.

After hearing about Bruno's past at the bar, I had seen the uncompromising justice he envisioned, and I believed his philosophy wasn't wrong. However, I hadn't wanted it to be the right answer. Bruno's concept of justice was so flawless it scared me.

After all, I'd had a partner like him. Someone who hadn't hesitated to lay down her own life.

"We sensed the danger in that consummate justice, and so we began to search for a way to bring about a new peace through a different approach. The key is to find a point of compromise. We'll strike a balance between justice and evil, order and chaos."

That mindset was just what I'd have expected from the pragmatic Stephen. As a doctor, he ultimately wanted to save the greatest number of lives, which meant he wouldn't touch patients if there was no hope of saving them.

"What is this method? What do we have to do to end this without hurting anyone?" As I asked Stephen the question, I realized deep down that I'd been looking for such a method this whole time myself.

It was like how Noel had prayed for Bruno's safety even as she tried to prevent the unknown crisis. I'd known this event would occur, but I hadn't really wanted Siesta and Nagisa to go back to being Ace Detectives.

Ever since the end of the Great Cataclysm, I'd had just one wish—for both detectives to have peaceful, happy lives. That was all.

"The only way to protect the world is this."

As Stephen spoke, a new shadow crept up to him.

"—We have only one request."

It was the thing in the crow mask, the one we'd encountered on the cruise. It gazed at me with those hollow eyes, its red robe flapping in the wind.

"We struck an independent deal with the messenger from Another Eden. Of course, the Federation Government is not involved."

"...A deal? What do they want?"

Another Eden had originally been trying to nail down some sort of treaty with the Federation Government. So they'd approached Stephen's group with a deal that would take the place of that one?

"*The origin text hidden in your jacket.* All we have to do is give them that, and this will be over." Stephen pointed at me, his keen eyes watching me from behind his glasses.

Had he known I possessed it when he called me here?

"Why the origin text, though? What do they want it for?"

"The origin text is supposed to have a special ability that will activate when it's given to the person who should rightfully possess it. Another Eden fears that the power will be used against them."

"The origin text wasn't what they asked the Federation Government for, though. Why the sudden change of heart?"

Even on the cruise ship today, the thing in the crow mask had asked for the world's secret. That couldn't actually be the text.

"That was the compromise we reached after discussing the matter. They've promised that as long as they have the origin text, they'll do no harm to the world."

This was hard to believe.

These were all just verbal promises. There was no guarantee they'd keep them. Besides…

"If we give them the origin text now, the Ritual of Sacred Return won't happen tomorrow. And then I won't get what I'm after."

If the ceremony wasn't held, the promise Noel had made me about letting Siesta and Nagisa leave the Tuners would fall through.

All I wanted was for the detectives' peace to be guaranteed after we headed off the unknown crisis.

"No—the Ritual of Sacred Return will proceed as planned. Use this." Stephen took a book from his bag.

"A second origin text…?"

No. This looked very similar, but it had to be a fake.

"Will it fool Mia? Even if you made it?"

"We won't need to fool the Oracle herself. We simply need to trick everyone else, and only temporarily. Think about it," Stephen told me. "Mia Whitlock intentionally gave that to you. It means she won't interfere with the choice you make."

"…You mean even if she realizes this is a fake, she'll accept it?"

"Yes. She must know that's her final job as the Oracle."

While hearing him out, I searched for a solid reason to reject Stephen's proposal.

If I gave them this book, what would happen? I visualized the potential threats and risks. Were those risks enough of a reason to refuse their request? —*Think.* I thought and thought, and finally, something I'd seen long ago crossed my mind.

"—I want to drink tea with you again, Kimi."

It was something the detective had said once. It had been her way of saying *I want to live.*

"Come to think of it, I haven't had any tea for a while."

Out of nowhere, I remembered that Siesta had looked a little lonely today.

Once we'd cleared up this incident, the three of us should go have a leisurely afternoon tea somewhere.

I heard a footstep. The thing in the crow mask had walked up to me.

"You want this that badly?"

My hand tightened on the origin text. No matter how I thought about it, I couldn't find a decent reason to turn down Stephen's proposal.

"People may call this a makeshift justice, but..."

Even so, if this made it possible to protect both the world and those two, then...

"We have a deal."

The turning point of fate left my hands.

In the moonlit temple, I'd chosen a future.

Side Noel

When the hands of the clock had nearly reached midnight, I knocked at the door of the mansion's guest room. "Come in," said a familiar voice.

"Excuse me."

When I opened the door, Bruno Belmondo was waiting for me. Since Grandfather had been invited to the Ritual of Sacred Return as a guest, I was having him stay at my house, a mansion administered by the Federation Government.

We'd lived as family, long ago, but now we were a host and her guest. The thought made an indescribable emotion threaten to well up inside me, and I gently pushed it down.

"You were out quite late."

Grandfather was just hanging up his overcoat. He smelled faintly of alcohol. Drinking was one of his many pastimes.

"Yes, I was with an acquaintance. We had a pleasant time," he explained simply.

He wouldn't tell me who he'd met or what they'd talked about.

It had always been that way. Grandfather never said much about himself.

Was it due to his position as the Information Broker, or was it—

"Grandfather, what's...?"

I'd noticed something that concerned me. On the table beside Grandfather, there was a half-empty bottle of water and something that looked like a medicine packet.

"Oh, it's my blood pressure medication. It's nothing to worry about."

"Grandfather? Are you sure you should be drinking?"

"…I'd rather you didn't mention it to my doctor." A little uncomfortable, Grandfather lightly raised one hand in a gesture of refusal.

It felt as if it had been a long time since I saw him do something that mischievous.

"And? What did you need?" Grandfather asked, as I hesitated in the doorway. "Is it about the ceremony tomorrow? If so, I really do intend to—"

"No, I know. You'd never abandon your mission."

Even if danger was bearing down on him, he'd prioritize the world's stability. That was how Bruno Belmondo the Information Broker lived. I understood that better than anyone.

"I'm sorry. I know I'm causing trouble for you," Grandfather said, giving me a faint smile.

"No, it's no trouble." *After all, you're family*, I started to say, but I promptly realized I wasn't qualified to anymore.

Silence fell. There were other questions I should ask, really, but the words wouldn't come. Grandfather gestured to a nearby chair, encouraging me to sit.

"…You know everything, Grandfather," I blurted out. It was just a fact. "You know about politics, finance, culture, and art. Sometimes you know futures even the Oracle can't see."

He probably knew things the Federation Government and I didn't know. And so… "I suspect you know what's going to happen tomorrow, don't you?" I stared down at my hands. "It's true, isn't it? If you are the all-knowing Information Broker, you know which way the world will tilt. That isn't all; you even know about those of us who will live in it…"

"Noel."

At the sound of my name, I looked up. Grandfather was smiling at me gently. He put his index finger to his lips. As I sat there, still and silent, he lowered himself into a chair at the table. The dim orange light threw shadows across his face.

Finally, polishing his usual cane with a cloth, Grandfather began to speak quietly. "I journeyed for a hundred years. In the most remote deserts and snowy mountains, I lived through the idle rumors you hear at run-down taverns. I discovered the sunken ruins of an ancient city, then found that an identical city had already been depicted in a certain best-selling novel.

Several unknown species I found in the heart of a jungle fifty years ago now appear in picture encyclopedias for elementary school students. Items of knowledge are isolated points," he told me. "In the space of a century, those points formed a line, becoming what the world considers common knowledge."

That was how he'd lived as the Information Broker, and how he'd interacted with the world as a Tuner. Long before I was sent to him to be fostered, Grandfather had been traveling the globe, accumulating knowledge, then returning that knowledge to the world as the occasion arose.

"I know things. I know everything—but within the boundaries the world has drawn up for me."

I hadn't been expecting that repudiation.

Grandfather knew everything, but...

"What humans know will never grow beyond what the world has established for them."

Grandfather was aware that his wisdom had limits.

"You mean there are things even the Information Broker doesn't know?" I asked.

He gazed into the distance—out the window, beyond the pall of night, to bygone days. It was probably a view I knew nothing of. "Once, my travels took me to a forbidden territory. While there, I made a choice. Should I know 'the world,' or everything else? I chose the latter."

What he was saying seemed very abstract. However, if I could believe his words, Grandfather had once chosen to know about everything except the world.

From another perspective, he was saying he'd given up on knowing the world.

What "world" did he mean?

"I may have said a bit too much. Liquor really should be taken in moderation."

With a little smile, Grandfather wrapped up his story. He'd never actually told me if he knew what was going to happen at tomorrow's ceremony.

But his story was the answer to my question. He'd said that Bruno Belmondo didn't know everything about the world.

Why had he done that? If it had been the Ace Detective asking, what answer would he have given her? My fingers tightened around my phone.

"Now then, children should be in bed around this time," Grandfather said, getting to his feet. He patted my head gently.

"...Honestly. I'm not a child."

He only did that at times like this—no, Grandfather had always treated me like a child. I didn't know whether that frustrated me or made me happy; I just stood there for a while, under his big palm.

The coolness of the wet towel he'd placed on my forehead when I was in bed with a cold. Camera film with sights from around the world on it. The warm hand that had held mine and led me along busy streets when I was small. Remembering these traces of Grandfather, I squeezed my eyes shut.

"I'm sorry to disturb you when you're tired." Rising from my chair, I nodded to him, then turned to go.

"Noel."

Just as I reached the door, Grandfather called to me. "Do as you see fit. We are humans of flesh and blood."

I didn't have a good response for that. "Good night," I told him, then closed the door.

Chapter 3

◆ At this train's final destination...

When I woke up at the hotel the next morning, I was the only one in the room.

"...Did they go out?"

Nagisa and Siesta had occupied those two empty beds when I went to sleep.

Last night, after talking things over with Stephen, I'd given the origin text to the messenger from Another Eden. When I'd gotten back to the hotel, Siesta and Nagisa were already in bed. However, Nagisa had heard me come in; she'd sat up and asked how my talk with Bruno had gone.

I told her I hadn't been able to convince him to stay away from the ceremony. I thought maybe I should tell her about meeting Stephen, too... but I wasn't sure I wanted to. In the end, I couldn't bring it up. Nagisa had seemed like she still had something she wanted to say, but I'd climbed into my own bed and shut my eyes.

"So this isn't going to be one of those 'They weren't actually all that mad' things?"

...Probably not. Siesta and I still hadn't made up over our argument at the bar yesterday. Nagisa had wanted to tell me something, but I hadn't let her do it. Maybe I was lucky they'd gone out; the morning could have been pretty awkward otherwise.

"Nah, I'll hurry and go meet up with them."

Then I'd tell them everything was all right now. That there was no need to worry about today.

Deciding to get changed and go look for them, I got out of bed, but then—

"The two detectives have only gone to have themselves formally dressed."

When I turned around, Noel de Lupwise was standing there. Instead of her earlier Gothic Lolita costume, she was dressed in an aristocratic gown, which was normal by comparison.

"That's not your Federation Government uniform."

"No. I've been tasked with running the ceremony and guiding people today."

Ah. So that was why she'd come to get me. "That aside, Noel, this is breaking and entering."

"I'm sorry. I'd intended to come a little earlier and wake you, but..."

That was not at all what she needed to apologize for.

"I'd meant to give a perfect performance as an admirable little sister who gently wakes her brother, but..."

Actually, I may be sorry I missed that.

"Heh-heh. That was a little sister joke." Noel smiled faintly.

So, she'd said Siesta and Nagisa had gone to get dressed up?

"Since there is a ball before the Ritual of Sacred Return, the female guests must begin their preparations a little early."

...Oh, was that why? Then they hadn't stormed out because they were furious with me?

"By the way, when I came to fetch those two, Miss Siesta looked more out of sorts than I've ever seen her. Did something happen yesterday?"

"So they're mad after all."

Damn. I was starting to want to see them less.

As my mood deflated, I sluggishly began getting ready to go out.

"The day has finally come." Apparently, Noel was planning to wait in the room with me, although she did have her back turned toward me. "Did you sleep well last night?"

"After that cruise, I drank a bit, so I slept like a rock."

"That's good. You met Grandfather again, didn't you?"

"Yes, I had the honor of drinking one-on-one with someone with the world's wisdom."

"You tried to persuade him again, then. Thank you very much."

Noel seemed to have a vague notion of what we'd talked about.

Talking hadn't changed anything, though: Bruno was still planning to attend the ceremony. That couldn't be what Noel wanted. She gazed out at the distant scenery from our room on the thirty-fifth floor. Reflected in the window, her eyes wavered uneasily.

"Mr. Kimihiko, if you knew there was a bomb on a train you were riding, would you stay on that train?"

What an abstract question. I didn't really get what she was trying to say, so I asked a few questions of my own.

"There's no telling when that bomb is going to explode?"

"No."

"Are we on that train of our own free will?"

"Yes."

"Is there a reason we absolutely have to reach our destination?"

"Yes."

In that case...

"I've been riding trains like that for years now."

Noel turned, waiting for me to go on.

"The fuse on that bomb was still lit, too. I thought it had gone out—or that I'd put it out—several times. And yet the next thing I knew, the flame was always right up close. There's no avoiding that, though. That proves how big my wish was."

I'd experienced trials, been tormented by its price, and even regretted making the wish at all—but that all meant the will behind it was strong.

"Is it all right for us to have our own selfish wishes?"

"Wishes can become more solid goals, and if you have one of those, you can take action. Without them, you can't pull yourself out of your routine."

It had been a long time ago now, but until I'd encountered Nagisa's boiling passion, I'd spent the year after Siesta died soaking in tepid routine.

"Then, wishing for something at the cost of something else isn't a bad thing?"

"It might not even have a shot of coming true until you're bad enough that you'd sacrifice anything for it."

A former enemy had told me as much before he died. He'd said if I didn't care what my wish cost, then I should keep moving forward. So even if the world called that evil, we'd—

"Thank you." Letting a faint smile suffuse her usual doll-like expression, Noel bowed her head to me. "Now, shall we go? I'll escort you to the venue."

"Yeah, please do."

Once I was dressed, I grabbed my bag, which had something precious in it.

The ceremony, in which many different intentions were at work, was about to begin.

◆ Tonight, justice gathers here

The venue for the ball turned out to be a magnificent, palatial building. From what Noel said, it was under the jurisdiction of the Federation Government, and Federal Councils sometimes took place here.

Inside, men in tuxedos and women in elegant gowns were already enjoying a buffet party. I spotted faces I thought I'd seen on TV in the crowd: politicians from somewhere or other, and members of industrial groups. If they'd been invited to this event, they must also be involved in the world's hidden dealings as well.

"Once again, the ball will begin at five o'clock, while the Ritual of Sacred Return will take place at seven. The ceremony itself is scheduled to take approximately thirty minutes, with a formal dinner to follow."

Handing me a welcome drink, Noel went over the evening's schedule with me.

Apparently, attendance at the opening ball wasn't mandatory. The main event was the Ritual of Safe Return.

"The venue has a security system, but there's no guarantee it will stop an attack by Another Eden. If it fails…"

"You'd like the Ace Detectives to help out?" I asked.

Noel nodded apologetically.

However, that was the promise I'd initially made with her and Bruno. It was the reason Siesta and Nagisa had temporarily reclaimed their authority as Tuners.

"Right. That's not a decision I can make, but if it happens, I'm sure they'll both give everything they've got to their missions."

Even as I told her that, I was praying it wouldn't happen... No, I trusted that it wouldn't. That was what I'd laid the groundwork for last night.

"...Thank you. All right, I'll take my leave for now. I must begin preparing for the ceremony." Noel bowed respectfully, then left the room.

In the hall, everyone was mingling and chatting. I was standing alone at loose ends. Weren't Nagisa and Siesta here yet? I looked around restlessly.

"—You're still dependent on Boss, aren't you, Kimihiko?" a voice behind me said.

There weren't too many people who called me by my first name—I knew who it was immediately.

"I like how you're ignoring the fact that you're the exact same way, Mia."

When I turned around, Mia looked away in a huff, pretending she didn't know what I meant.

Mia Whitlock, the Oracle, was a former Tuner. In that glamorous purple dress, she looked far more grown-up than she had when she'd shut herself up in her clock tower.

Somebody else looked up at me primly from the wheelchair Mia was pushing. "You're pretty insolent for someone who's just Rill's pet. You should only have eyes for your master."

This was another former Tuner: Reloaded, the Magical Girl. She wore a vivid orange gown that was a perfect match for her bright, cheerful personality.

"It's been a long time, Rill. I missed you."

"...If you missed Rill, you could have come to see her."

Possibly because I'd been more honest with her than she'd expected, Rill scratched at her cheek awkwardly.

Yeesh. I'd thought she'd yell at me if I dropped in for a casual visit.

"It's just the two of you? What happened to Olivia?" I asked Mia. I'd assumed her servant would be attending the ceremony as well.

"...Olivia left me to go greet everyone." Mia's resentful gaze was fixed on the distant Olivia. So she'd been abandoned while she was far from home? Pathetic, but cute.

"I've been trying to become one with the wall for a while now, but it's difficult."

Apparently, a couple years hadn't improved her communication skills any. That was actually a relief.

"You're seriously lucky Rill is here." Below Mia's line of sight, Rill crossed her arms proudly. "Otherwise, you'd be so lonely. Be grateful."

"Weren't you looking for me? You seemed happy to see me."

"Wha—? How dare you talk to your senior like that!"

"You may be older than me, but I've been a Tuner longer than you have."

"Hey! Kimihiko! This girl is as insolent as they come!" For a second, I worried Rill's head might actually start steaming. "She used to be so docile she couldn't even answer back!"

The two of them had been this incompatible since they'd first met. The one thing that had changed was that Mia now had no trouble talking back to Rill.

However, being incompatible didn't necessarily mean they didn't get along. The fact that Reloaded had trusted Mia with her wheelchair, which was basically part of her, was the strongest proof of that there could be.

"Did you come here by yourself, Rill?"

"Yes. The higher-ups are heartless, aren't they? They just sent Rill an invitation, then told her to get herself here," Rill complained. Mia shrugged, agreeing with her. "In this era, though, Rill can go anywhere as long as she has this wheelchair. In that sense, she's still free. Even if she does need a little help from other people."

Back when I met her, Rill never would have said that.

She'd changed. She'd fought many crises and found her own answer in the process.

"That said, she'd heard that former Tuners could bring a servant, so she did consider bringing you...briefly." Rill looked up at me.

I'd once worked as the Magical Girl's servant.

At the time, she'd needed me, and I'd needed her.

"Wow, that's a blast from the past."

"Yes... Now that Rill thinks about it, though, all she saw was the enemy." Reloaded began to talk about her past and our shared memories. Back then, the world still had enemies to be defeated and crises to overcome. "In those days, nothing scared her. Fear didn't even exist for her. She took up her staff and fought giant monsters and mages, and she felt no pain."

She'd been invincible, the Magical Girl said.

She wasn't exaggerating, either. How had Reloaded managed to be the brave, unrivaled Magical Girl? Because, back then, she— No, now probably wasn't the time to get into that.

"Still, she really was a hero. Back then, Rill lived as a magical girl. Even now, she's proud of that."

"Yeah, me too."

The days I'd spent as Reloaded's partner had shaped me, the person known as Kimihiko Kimizuka. If, as they say, people always make the future pay for the past, then I'd at least like everything besides the cost to carry over to the future as well.

"It's hard to believe it's already been a couple of years since then. Time flies." Comparing the past to the present again, Rill smiled.

The crisis-riddled past and the tranquil present.

"I'm glad things are peaceful now."

Watching the attendees enjoying the buffet party, Mia spoke quietly.

"Still, it's so peaceful that sometimes I wonder if it might not all be fake."

I couldn't find an appropriate response right away. "You saved the world, Mia."

It hadn't been just Mia and Rill. On that day, all the Tuners had—

"Yes, I know. I think I probably still can't quite believe it. The fighting ended so suddenly, and I was freed from my mission. I'd assumed it would last forever," Mia said.

Rill smiled; she seemed to have felt the same way.

"Still, I'm sure what we need to do now hasn't changed," Mia told us. By "we," she probably meant the people who protected the world.

Olivia had mentioned this earlier. Although she'd been released from her mission as a Tuner, Mia was traveling the world, observing it with her own eyes, preparing for unseen crises.

"My role may have ended, but my way of life hasn't changed... I shouldn't change it. It's how Boss taught me to live." Mia seemed to be trying to remind herself.

"Rill would like to say that's true for her as well, but she'll probably need to retire from being a hero." The former Magical Girl looked down at her legs, which no longer worked. "And so this time as well..." she murmured.

She probably knew about the unknown crisis, but she wasn't in any shape to be as reckless as she once was. That was the price she'd paid for staking her own pride and wish in the fight.

"Well, sure. You've grown up," I told her.

Rill tilted her head, puzzled. She hadn't retired because of her injured legs.

"Reloaded, you graduated from being a magical girl because you grew up."

For a moment, Rill's jewellike eyes wavered. And then... "Thank you." For the first time in ages, the master gave her familiar—her pet—a treat.

Even I thought I had a talent for being a faithful dog. I smiled wryly.

"What do you say? Want to come serve Rill again?"

"Well, that's a really tempting offer, but..."

My attention had shifted to two figures beyond Mia and Rill. The girls noticed and both glanced back, too.

The two detectives were there, looking radiant in their sparkling gowns, dramatic makeup, and special hairstyles for the occasion.

"Boss!" Mia ran up to Siesta, who was wearing blue.

"It's been a long time. You really should dress up more often, Mia. It suits you."

"...No, that's you, Boss. You're so cute." Mia was blushing faintly.

"She's acting totally different than she did with Rill." Rill was gazing at the two of them steadily.

Don't let it get to you. Humans relate to each other in lots of different ways.

"It's been ages, Rill," Nagisa said. She was dressed in red.

Rill blinked several times, then smiled at her. "Well, if it isn't Kimihiko's ex-girlfriend."

"~~~~~! He dumped you too, you know!"

Are all the women I know spoiling for a fight?

◆ Accomplices in peace

"Mia. Here."

After that, while Siesta and Nagisa were chatting with Rill, I took a certain object from my bag.

"...So you brought the origin text." Mia reached out with a hint of relief to take what I was holding.

"Why did you give this to me?" Before I handed it to her, though, I had some questions.

When Olivia had given me the origin text on the plane, she hadn't said much about their reasons. Why had Mia entrusted it to me, when it was something ordinary people weren't even allowed to touch?

"If I said I'd seen it in a dream, would you be angry?" Mia looked up at me, forcing a smile. She wasn't joking around, though, and she didn't seem to be trying to dodge the question.

"I can't see the future or predict global crises now, but for some reason, I was sure I had to give that book to you. I woke up one morning and thought, 'If nothing else, I have to protect that future.'"

Had it been a prophetic dream, or the Oracle's sixth sense, or some inevitability based more in fact than either of those things? If Mia herself didn't know, I couldn't press the issue.

However, I'd have to know the truth someday. This wasn't a hunch; the thought was founded on a kind of certainty.

"Mia, I'm sorry." I didn't even know whether apologizing was the right thing to do.

Mia looked puzzled, and I just handed her the book.

"—This is..." The moment she took it, she gave me a startled look.

She'd realized that it was a fake.

I had to keep my eyes on her, at least. I waited for the Oracle's verdict.

"I see. So this is your answer, Kimihiko."

Mia was the first to look away. She drew a deep breath, then hugged the false origin text to her chest and returned her gaze to me. "All right. If this is your choice, I'll accept it."

As Stephen had said, Mia had picked up on my plot, and chosen to ignore it.

She wasn't agreeing or disagreeing. She only seemed to be praying that this would be the correct future.

"Have you mentioned anything to Boss?"

"...No, not yet."

I hadn't intended to tell the detective about this wish, this secret, myself.

"You should talk it over. Most trouble between a couple is due to insufficient communication."

"Since when are you a romance guru?" I retorted.

Mia gave me a little smile. "Either way, I'll respect your decision. Let's make sure this ceremony succeeds." She held out her hand for a handshake.

As I reached for it, I realized that something was off.

Make sure this ceremony succeeds. Since the origin text was a fake, "success" in the truest sense of the word wouldn't be possible. Mia had to know that, so why...?

"I'm like you. I prefer stories with happy endings." There was a hint of melancholy in Mia's smile.

"—I see. You too."

Did she know where the real origin text had gone?

Stephen already made contact with Mia... Actually, he'd probably met with her before he'd seen me, and he'd tried to negotiate the transfer of the origin text at that time. Had Mia hesitated, then entrusted the origin text to me instead?

The Oracle had weighed the options, too. Flawless justice that didn't balk at waging war or making sacrifices, or peace based in a compromise that allowed evil to exist: Which should the world choose?

"Yeah, Mia. Let's do this together."

Mia and I shook hands.

Why hadn't I talked this over with the Ace Detectives? Because for all of us, it was something that went without saying.

In this moment, we were accomplices.

Soon after that, Olivia came to pick up Mia, and the two of them and Rill went off to see another group of acquaintances. The former Tuner who'd traveled the world might not be a good communicator, but she seemed to know a lot of people anyway.

Then Nagisa, Siesta, and I were the only ones there.

When one of us seemed about to make eye contact with another, both would look away. We all knew we'd argued and failed to find common ground; that was why the mood was so awkward. We also understood that this fight had been on a different level from our usual arguments.

"Haaah. There's just no helping us, is there? Geez." Nagisa cracked first. Sighing, she turned to me. "Kimihiko, what are you going to do about you-know-what?" Just in case, she lowered her voice, very conscious of the people around us.

"You-know-what" was a maneuver the three of us had been setting up in secret ever since we'd arrived in France. After hesitating, I told her, "Let's cancel it."

Nagisa's eyes widened a little. "If I asked you why, could you tell me here?"

"...I don't think so. I have an idea, though."

She pressed her lips together, watching me steadily. It was as if she suspected I was trying to cover something up... No, I think she was worried by that possibility.

"All right. That's fine." Surprisingly, Siesta was next to speak. "Remember what I said at the hotel yesterday afternoon? We're letting Kimi give the orders this time."

"I thought the fight last night had reset all of that."

"I'm not a child, you know. I don't let my emotions control me. Are you stupid, Kimi?" Siesta pouted.

"Huh? Am I remembering yesterday wrong? When we got back to the hotel from the bar, all the way until we went to bed, you kept fixating on the fact that you'd fought with Kimihiko and getting mad, then depressed, like a little kid."

"Nagisa, that wasn't necessary." Siesta gave Nagisa a long, even look, then turned back to me. "Let's assume this conversation has evaporated from your memories, Assistant."

"Yeah, it's gone. I don't remember a thing, so don't worry," I joked.

Siesta smiled. "I want to see the answer you've found for this story."

She held out her left hand to me. Was this a "Let's make up" handshake? If so, that really was way too childish. Ignoring her hand, I gave her a wry smile instead.

"The ball's about to start," Nagisa said, looking around. The tables had been cleared of their drinks and refreshments, and couples were standing here and there in the open space, chatting.

"And? Which of us will you dance with, Kimihiko?" Nagisa asked, pressing me to choose.

Would I dance with Siesta, or with Nagisa?

"It's not like I can't dance with both of you, is it?"

"But it matters whose hand you'll take first."

Geez, this was a tough one. As I was stressing out over the world's hardest question…

"Sorry. I have a previous engagement," Siesta said. She turned away, gown flaring. As she did, she glanced at me, and the corners of her lips rose very slightly. Maybe this was payback for last night.

"She really is a kid." I shrugged, turning my back on Siesta. "…Oh, she's dancing with Mia, huh?"

"Lame. Don't immediately check to see who she's dancing with." Nagisa retorted, dragging my eyes back to her. "Were you worried her partner might be another guy?"

"Not even possible. I'm not in middle school. I'm not even in high school anymore."

"Hmm. Well, as long as you understand that."

Yeah, we were all adults. When I looked at Nagisa, dressed to the nines, there was no way I could think otherwise.

Then the music started, and the ball began.

Nagisa and I gazed at each other. I gently took her hand. "We're the only ones left. Want to dance?"

"Hmm. By process of elimination?"

"…Sorry; that was the wrong approach. May I have this dance, Nagisa?"

Nagisa smiled, then leaned in toward me. "The other way's fine, too." She was wearing heels, so her face was right in front of mine. Her beautiful red eyes watched me steadily. "As long as you'll look at me. Even if it's only for now, or when you're not sure what to do."

◆ The result of searching for the credits

After the ball ended, just before seven, we all relocated to the venue for the Ritual of Sacred Return.

It was a large, oval hall with a retractable roof, built to accommodate several thousand people. That and the screen at the front made it look like a concert venue.

"Your seats are this way."

The hall was about a third full.

Noel led Nagisa, Siesta, and I to our seats in a row near the back.

"I hope you enjoyed the ball." Noel took a seat beside me. From this point on, she'd just be attending the ceremony like the rest of us.

"How does it look? Has anything weird happened?"

"No, not particularly. Security is being kept very tight as well."

"I see," I said, nodding. Everything was going smoothly so far. However, if something was going to happen…

"The rest depends on the Ritual of Sacred Return, then," Siesta said, gazing at the stage at the front of the hall. There was a large, white pillar on the stage, with firewood piled in front of it as if they were planning to have a bonfire. Was that going to be used in the ritual? It was almost like an altar.

"It should begin in about five minutes," Noel told us, checking the time.

When I looked out over the hall, I spotted Bruno sitting in a seat toward the front on the right, near a door. Troops under the direct command of the Federation Government—a force known as the White Suits—were stationed around him. Although they weren't Tuners, they were an elite group that had helped to resolve conflicts and incidents all over the world. They'd been stationed here to protect Bruno.

The world's wisdom is about to perish. We still didn't know who had sent that letter. Either way, the unknown crisis wouldn't happen here. I'd shut it down by making that contract yesterday.

"Is that Mia sitting over there?" Nagisa pointed at a seat in the front, a special bench that stood out from the rest.

I couldn't see clearly from this angle, but I did make out something like the Oracle's costume sticking out past the edge of the seat. There was a figure standing nearby; from its height, I assumed it was Olivia.

"Yes. The Oracle has a special part to play in the ritual."

"Oh, that's right... Aside from us, though, there are hardly any Tuners here."

As Nagisa said, the only other Tuner I saw was Rill, over in a reserved wheelchair space. Naturally, Fuubi Kase, the former Assassin, wasn't here.

"True. The Men in Black are guarding the venue and its perimeter, but no other former Tuners are in attendance."

The Men in Black were a large organization, and they'd once worked as handymen for the other Tuners. They always wore dark suits and sunglasses; even now, we didn't know any of their real faces. However, the idea that they were protecting this place made me feel a little safer.

"Stephen really isn't here, is he? There was something I wanted to talk to him about..." Siesta said.

I actually knew where Stephen and quite a few other former Tuners had gone. I couldn't say so here, though.

After a couple more minutes, we heard the low sound of a bell.

"It's starting."

Noel faced forward. That bell had signaled the beginning of the Ritual of Sacred Return. Over our heads, the roof opened to reveal a starry sky. Then, a dozen masked, costumed individuals filed in through two doors near the front of the hall.

"Those are government dignitaries."

It was impossible to tell their ages or genders. They seated themselves in a row at the very front, beside Mia.

Technically, Noel's title qualified her to be up there, too. However, she'd told us that she'd acquired her position suddenly through hereditary succession, and due to her lack of experience, she was only ever assigned servant-type work.

Several of the officials rose to their feet. One blew an instrument that looked like a conch shell, while two others walked to the stage and lit the stack of firewood. In front of the pillar, pale flames began to climb into the night sky.

For a little while, the hall was silent. Then someone I knew very well stood up: Mia Whitlock, the girl in the Oracle's costume. She and her servant Olivia ascended the stairs together, and she began feeding the sacred texts she was handed into the flames.

"After this ritual, Mia will have completely lost her abilities as the Oracle, correct?" said Nagisa. "...Will that really be enough to end all disasters? She'll burn the origin text, returning her power. What if she does all that, and then there's another global crisis? I'm not sure that doing this guarantees we'll be all right."

As she spoke, the flames crawled across several more volumes of the sacred text.

"Yeah, the Ritual of Sacred Return has been performed several times throughout history, and the results have been self-evident," I answered for Noel. "Not that peace will be permanent," I added.

Nagisa's eyes widened.

"...So you noticed, Mr. Kimihiko." Noel gave a small nod. She seemed vaguely resigned.

Yesterday in the car, Noel had said that the effects of the Ritual of Safe Return were guaranteed by several millennia of records. If the ritual had been held in the past, the world should have been peaceful already, but we'd instead run into all those global crises.

It was likely that this was a cycle, something that had been repeated for the past several thousand years. Why did they still need to hold this ritual? Why didn't they learn? And if all of this was true, why had Noel been able to declare that our peace and safety would be guaranteed? It was because—

"There's a limit to the peace the ritual brings, isn't there?" I asked.

"Two hundred years," Noel said, gazing at the distant white smoke. "After a Ritual of Sacred Return is held, there will be no global crises for at least two centuries."

Two centuries. At the very least, the next disaster wouldn't happen for another two hundred years.

Essentially, *the safety of people living in this particular era was guaranteed*.

"It may be a fleeting peace in the grand scheme of the world, but it is a lasting peace for humans."

Another disaster was bound to occur someday, but not before the end of our natural lives. Had the world done this over and over for thousands of years?

In that case...

"That was the right choice."

It didn't matter whether we burned the real origin text or the false one. The world wouldn't gain lasting peace either way. My choice—the choice Stephen's group had made—could prevent the unknown crisis now. It had been the right call.

"There they go," Siesta murmured, watching the ritual.

All the crises that had assailed the world were being consigned to the sacred flames, sublimated into smoke that rose high into the sky.

In the meantime, one of the Federation Government officials rose from their seat and read from a scroll. It was a poem praising those who'd fought to protect the world, one that showed a determination to defend the coming peace.

It wasn't that the words themselves had any value. The poem was in a foreign language, so I didn't even understand all of it, but I closed my eyes and listened. It made me think of the past.

We'd spent those days running desperately; we'd lost so much, but we'd kept reaching out for the wishes we'd wanted to come true. And we'd won. We'd reached our happy ending. All the fighting was over, and these days, no one cried.

"*—Are you sure?*"

I thought I heard a voice.

Who had whispered those words to me recently?

"Kimihiko?" Nagisa was watching me worriedly.

"It's nothing," I said, shaking my head, and just then—

Bang! A gunshot echoed through the hall.

Bright red blood spattered the white pillar of the altar.

"Madame Mia!"

A frantic scream rang out—it was Olivia.

Up on the stage, she rushed toward the young Oracle, who crumpled into her arms.

Justice had been defiled by an assassin's bullet.

"Enemy attack!"

There was no telling who had been the first to scream those words. A second later, confusion erupted in the hall. The one thing anyone knew for sure was that the Oracle had been shot.

"...Mia."

Up on the distant altar, Mia lay limp in Olivia's embrace. Her shoulder was bleeding. In my mind's eye, I saw the smile she'd given me before the ceremony when she'd told me she liked happy endings, too.

"What's going on?"

Something was wrong. Why was this happening?

My mind had gone into overdrive, but it wasn't giving me any answers. The only words I could find were a complaint, one so stupid I would rather have died than said it aloud: *It wasn't supposed to be like this.*

"It can't... That's ridiculous..."

No—the future I'd wished for hadn't ended like this. The crises should have been gone.

Who was it? Who had sold us out?

Was it Stephen? That thing in the crow mask? Or had it been—

"Siesta, wait!" Nagisa launched herself into a run.

Someone had started moving even before she did.

As Nagisa reached out for her, the white-haired detective had taken off like a shot. Grabbing her musket from under the seats, she rushed toward Mia like a gust of wind.

But Siesta hadn't noticed that she was being targeted as well.

"—Siesta, watch out! Second-floor seats, opposite side!"

The thing in the crow mask was up there, leveling a black rifle. Siesta heard me through her earpiece, but by the time she saw the enemy and gasped, the shot had already been fired.

A bullet moving faster than the speed of sound was headed straight for her. There was no time to dodge. In other words—

"Siesta…!"

A spray of blood bloomed like a flower. Siesta staggered, then fell over without even trying to catch herself.

"……!"

The next thing I knew, I was in motion. I'd started running before I could put my feelings into words like *It's too late. Even if I get there, there's no point.* I was swimming upstream through the crowd, bumping into people. Everyone was screaming something, but weirdly, I couldn't hear their voices.

It was like the sound had cut out.

I couldn't see anything in color. Then, just as I hit the bottom of the stairs, my sense of balance deserted me, and I collapsed to the floor. I stretched out my hand, trying to reach Siesta's distant, motionless shape.

"Sie…sta…"

I knew. I recognized this scene.

That's right. On that day, just like this, the detective had—

"Again…?"

This ending was wrong. I'd been obsessed in my pursuit of a future where things didn't turn out like this. Even so, it was my fault this had happened. I'd gotten something wrong. In that case, I—

"_____!"

Just then, I saw someone run to Siesta, screaming.

It was Nagisa. The other detective sprinted, driven by her passion.

I watched her back until she reached Siesta, then blacked out.

A certain young man's choice

What had I gotten wrong?

I didn't even really have to ask. I already knew. However, I was reluctant to say it aloud, so I walked down the dark street in silence, all by myself.

"A street at night?"

Where was I? Where was I trying to go?

I had to get back. I had to go to Siesta. What was I doing here—?

"You already know that, too, don't you?" someone whispered.

I looked down the street and saw a black shadow stretching from beneath a streetlight.

The person casting that shadow was the one who'd spoken. His name was…

"—Scarlet."

His yellow eyes glowed ominously in the dark. A pale devil who drank human blood—a vampire. I hadn't thought I'd ever see him again.

"What's this—another dream?"

It wasn't just any dream, either. It was a nightmare that would leave me feeling like shit when I woke up.

"You're that unhappy to see me, human?" Scarlet said, addressing me by the same careless label he'd always used.

"If I told you I was glad to see you, what would you do?"

"I would determine that some scoundrel had assumed your identity and would immediately rip out his throat."

"I'm glad you didn't get any weird ideas, then. Let's keep this peaceful."

For several seconds, Scarlet and I stayed silent, letting our eyes do the talking. We didn't need words to discuss this reunion of ours.

"And? Do you know where we are, Scarlet?"

We were in a dark world, with one street reaching into the distance. Scarlet was leaning against a streetlamp, the only source of light. "I couldn't say. However, even if I don't know, you should."

"Is that a Zen koan?"

"That would do as well. Now, answer my question, human," Scarlet said. "Where did you go wrong? What mistake has left you stagnating here?"

Oh, so that was what this was. He was going to keep me company while I asked myself dumb questions. Had that been why Scarlet was waiting here? In that case...

"I guess the world we live in won't stand for anything that's been done by half measures." I was talking as much to myself as to Scarlet. "It wouldn't allow fleeting peace or counterfeit justice. It forced me to confront reality again. It won't free the Tuners from their mission so easily. It won't let them run from a fight."

That was why I'd failed. I'd tried to get the Ace Detectives out of that brutal world, and some invisible demon's hand had grabbed us by the ankles. We were left powerless. We'd never had a choice.

"Having an enemy you must fight is a truly pleasant thing, isn't it?" Scarlet looked up into the pitch-black sky. "The more formidable that foe, the better. An evil so great that you can claim your wishes will never come true so long as it exists. If, as you say, the world itself is your enemy, nothing could be better."

"...It's the other way around. It's not better if the wall between us and our wishes is larger."

It sounded like he was saying that if I was going to climb a wall anyway, higher was better—but that couldn't have been right.

"No, I'm talking about humanity's bad habit." Scarlet's tone grew harsher. "When humans cause a problem, you always dream up some outside enemy and try to find the cause in them. Then you say, 'They're to blame. That enemy is the reason we're suffering.' Fighting a great foe really is the easiest option," Scarlet said. "People are intoxicated by the concept of themselves locked in combat with a mighty evil. Even if they yield to that evil, they comfort each other with loud declarations that they fought well. If your wish doesn't come true because the world itself is your enemy, then you can be satisfied that another outcome wasn't possible."

"Are you trying to say I'm actually satisfied with this? That I've accepted it? A reality where Mia and Siesta get gunned down?"

"No. You are not, and that is why you are here. Isn't it?" Scarlet began to walk in a circle around me, his shoes clicking on the pavement. "While most humans are satisfied with their powerful enemies and meet with defeat, you are trying to deny that reality. You've come here to redo a certain choice."

...He was right. I wanted to try again. I wanted to go back to before that tragedy occurred and choose a different future, but that would mean...

"Does that mean I have to reject a world where the Tuners live in peace?"

If the events of that ceremony had happened because I'd wished for a world where they could be free of their missions, then changing that fate meant placing their heavy mission as Tuners on their shoulders again. Either way, Siesta and the rest would...

"Kimihiko Kimizuka, you must have realized how fragile a fleeting peace is."

Yeah, I had. Wishing for it was what had gotten us that terrible ending.

"I just wanted Siesta and Nagisa to live in peace. That was the only wish I had. And so—"

"I do not believe that you are lying. However," Scarlet whispered in my ear, "remove your armor. No doubt there's another emotion hidden inside it."

I was taken aback.

Scarlet laughed a little. "Do you think it's odd for me to express my opinions on human emotions?"

No, I didn't.

After all, I knew who had made him able to say those things.

"Come, it's time you woke from your nightmare." Scarlet thumped me lightly on the shoulder. "You know what you must do, correct?"

"...Yeah. I do now."

I was holding a certain book in my hand. *Just as I had that other time, I'd use the power hidden in this volume.* This time and place had been here to make me remember that.

"Scarlet." He'd already turned his back on me, but I called to him one last time. "I'll believe in the world I managed to protect from you just a little longer."

Scarlet laughed. "You have quite a mouth these days... Still, if you ever get truly disgusted with this world, come to hell anytime. And bring my bride with you."

With that, the vampire melted into the darkness.

"Sorry, but that day's never gonna come," I murmured. My hands tightened on the origin text, and I set off again.

...Toward the future? No, not that way.

The road I was walking led to the past.

"I'm going to do it over, one more time."

I'd start on the night I'd made that choice.

And I'd make sure we ended up on the correct route this time.

Chapter 4

◆ The light of passion

The first time I'd encountered the origin text's special power had been yesterday, when Olivia had handed it to me on the plane.

When I took it, *I'd been able to see the future.*

It had felt like a really vivid dream, or an extremely specific sixth sense. Things that were probably going to happen had raced through my brain like a jolt of electricity.

In that dream, I'd refused to take the origin text, believing someone like me shouldn't accept it casually.

Olivia had been perplexed, but she'd kept the book and returned to her normal duties… But then our plane hadn't made it to France. Olivia had been attacked and wounded by somebody onboard, and we'd made an emergency landing at a nearby airport.

And—someone had stolen the origin text.

"I was wrong."

Not accepting the origin text had been a mistake. I regretted it fiercely, and the next thing I knew, I was back on the plane. Olivia was standing in front of me, and once again, the origin text was firmly in my hands.

At first, I hadn't understood what had happened. I'd asked Olivia if she was all right, then checked the time with Nagisa, only to find out that no time had passed at all.

I've returned to the past, I thought.

When I thought it over later on, though, I realized I hadn't time traveled— I'd just seen the future.

In other words, *when the origin text's bearer wasn't sure what to do about a major decision, it would show them the futures that would result from their various choices.* Since it was similar to the Oracle's clairvoyance, I deduced that I'd basically been borrowing Mia's power.

I immediately thought, *I shouldn't tell anybody about this yet.* If it was information I should share with Siesta and Nagisa, Mia would have told me so to begin with, and she hadn't. She hadn't even told Olivia. She probably thought I should be the only one to know about this power. Therefore, since Mia was the text's rightful owner, I respected her wishes.

I had one other concern, though: It was possible that even Mia wasn't aware of the origin text's true power. If so, I wasn't even sure I should ask her about it. As a result, I'd decided to take a little more time to observe the book closely.

I'd walked around with it for a while, but nothing odd had happened. I'd experimented by hesitating over a minor choice, trying to see any futures related to it, but the origin text's power hadn't activated. Either it would only show futures related to major turning points, or I wouldn't necessarily be able to use it whenever I wanted.

The next time the origin text had shown me the future had been last night, after I'd argued with Siesta and talked with Bruno. The turning point had been whether I would meet with Stephen or Nagisa. I'd chosen the former and let go of the origin text. I'd tried to protect the detectives' ordinary lives by choosing a transient peace. I don't have to tell you how that went.

—And so…

"I'll do it over."

On that dark road where I'd met Scarlet, in a gap in space-time, I made my decision. However, strictly speaking, I was returning from the future to the present. I'd cancel the potential future where Mia and Siesta were sniped by an assassin and choose another one.

Right at my feet, the path forked in two. On one route, I met Stephen and gave the origin text to the messenger from Another Eden, but I'd already seen where that would end up. As a result, I now chose the route where I went to meet Nagisa instead. Besides, in that first future, Nagisa had told me something:

When you're not sure what to do, look at me.

I'd put my trust in those words now. Nagisa had run to the fallen Siesta at the end of that future. This time, I'd chase after her.

"I'll start over from here."

I started down the second route. Soon, light enveloped me, and the next thing I knew, I'd returned to the previous night.

That means the story starting now happened right after I'd parted ways with Bruno at the pub.

This is the world where I didn't answer that call from Stephen, and chose to meet Nagisa instead.

"…Sorry to keep you waiting. Brrrr, it's cold."

It was a starry winter night, and we were in a park with a view of the illuminated Eiffel Tower.

Huddled up in her coat, Nagisa arrived at our meeting spot. I was waiting for her with my collar turned up against the cold.

I told her I'd met Bruno and summarized what we'd talked about. From my perspective, this was the second time I'd done this, but that was inevitable. When she heard I hadn't managed to persuade Bruno not to attend the ceremony, Nagisa sighed. "I see… Still, we could have talked about this at the hotel. It didn't have to be here."

"If I went back to the room now, Siesta would just be griping about me."

"Huh? How did you know? —Wait, ignore that, she's not doing anything of the sort."

Her eyes were darting around way too much. She'd been the one to tell me about that in the first place.

"Sure, she was a little angry, but I think she was more bewildered than anything." With a little smile, Nagisa told me what Siesta had been like right after we'd fought. "'Why won't my assistant understand?' she said. 'I'm only doing my job as the Ace Detective.'"

"…True. She's probably in the right, here. I'm wrong."

"Wow, that's unusual. Want to hurry back and apologize, then? I think she'll forgive you pretty easily."

"I can't do that." Nagisa looked perplexed, so I explained. "I want her to get it wrong, too."

Siesta's sense of justice was too correct. She wouldn't hesitate to keep fighting to protect the world and the people around her, no matter the personal cost. She'd tried to go to sleep forever once—twice—to that end. Now that the disasters had finally ended, the chain of tragedies had halted, and the world was at peace, I wanted her to throw that approach away.

"She was becoming more and more like who she used to be, wasn't she?"

So Nagisa had noticed, too? My sigh came out misty white as I gazed at the distant tower.

Two weeks ago, when the Federation Government had summoned us, and Noel had requested that she become a Tuner temporarily, Siesta had begun to revert to her old self.

Once she'd learned about the unknown crisis, she'd agreed to become a proxy Ace Detective. After that, she'd met Ms. Fuubi, remembered events from when she was a Tuner, and encountered someone who resembled an enemy she'd once fought. Picking up her musket again had reminded her of the sensations of being on the battlefield, and she'd asked Charlotte to do maintenance on the weapon for her.

The danger to Bruno had given Siesta an even greater sense of responsibility as the Ace Detective, and our encounter with Another Eden on the cruise ship had made her mission more real than ever... I couldn't help but worry about that. The Ace Detective's justice was too flawless.

"What about you? Did it make you remember old times, too, Nagisa?"

Naturally, Siesta wasn't the only one I was worried about.

Nagisa Natsunagi, the other detective, had also sacrificed herself to save Siesta once. She'd tried to return her heart to its former owner, to revert the world to what it should have been. She'd said it was because she was only a proxy detective.

"I never forgot."

"...You mean you haven't changed at all since then?"

The proxy detective who'd sacrificed herself.

"Yes. But listen, I haven't forgotten how kind you were to me that time, either." Nagisa's ruby eyes were blazing brightly. "You got angry, and you cried. I believed I was doing the right thing, and you said I wasn't. All of that makes me who I am now. That's why I've never forgotten. I was right *and* wrong, both at once. I'm sure it's the same for Siesta," she said.

So my feelings had reached her? Did Siesta remember, too? That was why, like me, she wasn't sure what to do.

"You know, Kimihiko, you always did like the detective way too much. You still do." Smiling, Nagisa stepped in closer. For some reason, she put the muffler she'd been wearing around my neck. Then she tied it up and gave it a tug. "Take that!"

"Hey, that hurts."

"Our positions have been flipped pretty much all the time lately, so I thought I'd remind you who's boss once in a while."

"Yeah. Three years ago, just for that one moment, you were a total sadist."

"J-just for that moment? Oh, come on… You make it sound like I've been a masochist the rest of the time."

Nagisa looked unhappy with that, but it was way too late to correct the trajectory of her character now.

"Say, Kimihiko?" Her tone turned a little serious again. "What did I look like before?"

For a moment, I didn't understand what she was asking.

In another moment, I realized she meant the old stories I'd brought up earlier.

"Your memories are precious to you, Kimihiko. How did Siesta and I smile in those memories? How did we look when we were angry, or when we cried? How did we shine?"

Of course. The detectives hadn't smiled all the time.

Our journeys hadn't been all fun and games. We'd gotten into plenty of dangerous scrapes, and we'd made it through life-or-death situations many times.

And on the other side, the detectives' faces had been flooded with fierce emotion; they'd looked…

"Kimizuka." Natsunagi called me by the name she'd addressed me by back then. "Which versions of us did you like?"

I'd… Back then, I'd—

"No, that's not it." Nagisa put her index finger to my lips before I could speak. "Now isn't the time or the place. I'm not the one you should be saying that to, either."

"...Yeah, you're right. I'll hang on to it for now."

Nagisa smiled and gave a little nod.

"Well, should we head back?"

A look at the clock told me it was almost eleven. *Tomorrow's a big day; we should probably hit the sack as early as possible*, I thought, turning around. Out of nowhere, someone caught my hand.

Needless to say, it was Nagisa.

"I'm sorry. I shouldn't have talked like I knew everything." Her forehead thunked lightly against my back.

"What are you talking about? You gave me plenty of strength," I told her. For as long as I'd known her, Nagisa had always said the words I wanted to hear. It was something she could do because she never let the fires of her passion die.

"No. I was speaking as the detective earlier. I'm going to say what I really think now." She kept her forehead pressed against my back. "I'm sorry for always making you do the worst parts. I'm sorry for shoving the decisions onto you. Thank you for trying to give us peace."

Her voice was slightly choked up.

"There were things that scared me, really. Fighting with my life on the line, long ago. The Great Cataclysm. We're on the cusp of getting involved in all this again now. And you're trying to save me, so..."

"...Stop it."

I was in no position to have Nagisa thank me. How many times had her words saved me, spurred me to act, made me look forward? Wishing she and Siesta could live peaceful, ordinary lives wasn't my repaying a favor. As a matter of fact, it was just my own ego. That meant Nagisa didn't owe me any gratitude.

"No, that won't do. At least one person has to acknowledge you out loud, Kimihiko. I bet Siesta's clumsy, so I'll say it. Thank you. Thank you for being our assistant, and our greatest partner."

Nagisa's voice, and her forehead, grew warmer.

Right now, those tears were what concerned me more than anything.

"Yeesh. I promised I wouldn't make you cry."

Hel would yell at me in my next dream. Turning around, I unwrapped the muffler and rewound it around its owner's neck. "I don't need apologies or thanks. I want you and Siesta to live in peace because…I like you two way too much, that's all. So don't worry about it."

I was aware I was saying one of "those" lines, but I told her anyway. That proved I'd grown up a bit.

Nagisa looked at me, startled. Her mouth hung open slightly. Her fingers dug into the muffler a bit as she averted her flushed face and found something to criticize.

"That was lousy." Apparently I needed more practice at putting mufflers on girls.

Then, something bright caught my attention at the corner of my vision. "Hm. That's pretty." The Eiffel Tower was lit up differently now. Come to think of it, I'd heard it flashed like this every hour after sunset for just five minutes.

"Well, Nagisa? Since you got to see this view, will you overlook the fact that I made you come out in the cold to meet me?" I joked, but just as I was about to turn back to her, something hot and soft touched my left cheek.

Nagisa had kissed me.

"…That's appreciation for all your hard work, all right?"

As her lips left my cheek, a hot sigh escaped them.

"A gesture of gratitude from a detective to her assistant, who always does his best. That's all it is. And so…" Nagisa covered her mouth with her muffler. "If you get the wrong idea, I'll half-kill you."

Compared to her usual counterstrikes, that one was pretty weak.

◆ Because it was a fleeting dream

When I woke up at the hotel the next morning, I was the only one in the room. I knew why the other two beds were empty, though, so I didn't worry about it.

After I'd talked with Nagisa last night, the two of us had gone back to the hotel where we were staying. As a result, my covert meeting with Stephen and his group hadn't happened.

Even so, everything else was proceeding as it had before. Before long,

Noel came to pick me up, and we headed for the palace where the ceremony would be held.

Once again, I ran into Mia and Rill there, and we had the same lively conversation we'd had in the other future. It would have been great if I'd been able to say something more tactful to Rill, but I'd save that for our next meeting. I'd probably be seeing her again.

The main thing after that was to return the origin text to Mia. Unlike in the other future, I hadn't given it to the thing in the crow mask.

I gave her the real origin text this time.

While Siesta and Nagisa chatted with Rill, I had my conversation with Mia.

"I see. So this is your answer, Kimihiko," Mia said. It was exactly what she'd said the other time. However, I was sure those words meant something different now.

"Are you sure this is what you want?" she asked me, hugging the origin text to her chest. The fact that it had returned to her was proof positive that the deal with Another Eden had fallen through. It was true that she'd left the decision in my hands, but her heart had to have been leaning in one direction or the other.

"Flawless justice and a transient peace," I murmured. Mia's shoulders jumped slightly. "I don't know which is the right choice, and which is the mistake. It's not for me to know."

I doubted I was qualified to decide a thing like that. Besides, even if an answer did turn up someday, that time would not be now.

"The question should keep until this ceremony's over, at least."

Until then, I'd keep fighting for just a little longer.

"...All right. I'll help."

We shook hands for the second time. This handshake meant something a bit different from our first, but I don't think we could have gotten here without the other one.

"Oh, right. Mia, I've got one other thing to tell you..."

A little while after that, Mia and Rill left, and then Siesta, Nagisa, and I were on our own. It was the same situation that had happened in the other future. Once again, the atmosphere was awkward beyond words...but not everything was the same as before.

"Siesta, please dance with me at the ball," I said, forestalling her right off the bat. We were still fighting. We hadn't exchanged two words since last night.

Siesta looked dubious. "Why me? Besides, I promised Mia I'd dance with—"

"I had Mia bow out. Unfortunately, I'm the only partner you've got."

"What's with the weird advance arrangements? Actually—Nagisa, you're okay with this?"

"Oh, it's fine. Kimihiko and I had fun in a park last night."

"Huh? Are you trying to one-up me? What were you people doing while I was asleep?" Siesta stared at Nagisa incredulously.

However, Nagisa just gave a little smile, waved, and left. As she passed me, she whispered, "The rest is up to you."

The music began. I held out a hand to Siesta, who was just standing there woodenly. Sighing, she took it.

"Okay. Let's go."

Clasping Siesta's hand, I put my other hand on her waist.

It was the inverse of our usual situation. I wasn't ordinarily the one who took her hand. After all, Siesta was always catching mine and pulling me along before I knew it.

"Can you dance, Kimi?"

"Do I look like I can?"

"No, not at all."

Don't say that with a straight face. Letting the music carry me, I muddled through a few steps by mimicking other people. "...Actually, Siesta, you lead."

The graceful dancing of everyone around us was making me wish I could disappear.

"Haaah. If I must," Siesta sighed. Pulling my hand, she drew me in close. I was pressed against her curves, and I could feel her body heat. With her in the lead, I managed to find the natural movements for my feet.

It wasn't as if we'd swapped gender roles. To bystanders, it probably even looked as though I was leading her. Siesta and I twirled like a carousel through the waltz—and then, out of nowhere, I felt eyes on me.

"We're being watched." Siesta gave an alluring smile. That low-cut gown, her elegant hairstyle, her formal makeup. She'd grown up, and just for the moment, I forgot everything else and danced with her.

"Are you embarrassed to have all these people focused on you?"

Not even possible.

I was proud. Right now, she was the center of the world.

"I'm sorry," I said, looking her in the eye.

"What are you apologizing for?" Siesta averted her eyes slightly.

"I've been remembering the past. Thinking about how we might have gotten our wires crossed like that." I didn't answer her question right away. Instead, I looked for the words that would get me there. For detectives and their assistants, theories needed to come before conclusions.

"Ever since we left on that first journey, we've fought quite a bit over quite a few things."

"You're reminiscing about our travels, and you start by remembering the fights?"

Well, I didn't feel great about that, either, but they were what came to mind first.

"Still, you're right. You always did things that made me mad. A simple week of sleeping outdoors left you grumpy, and when I suggested going to buy new weapons, you didn't look like you were having fun. When I slept soundly until noon, you'd wake me up."

"Those were brand-new hurdles for me, and you set them way too high." And that last one was completely not my fault. "The extraordinary stuff you brought into my life kept almost killing me."

"Yes, and I protected you so that it wouldn't happen. Over and over."

"Yeah... And every time you did, you put yourself in danger."

Siesta looked away again.

Even as we danced, we remembered those relentless days.

"Come to think of it, you got mad at me, too, Kimi. You said I'd damn well better look after you until the very, very, very end. You said that meant I couldn't go off and die without telling you." With a self-mocking smile, Siesta looked up at me again. "Did you hate that side of me?"

"Yeah, I did."

That was why, when the seed had begun to eat away at her heart and she'd tried to disappear, we'd fought with each other again. I'd wanted her to be more selfish. More than the world, more than the rest of us, I'd wanted her to value herself.

"I thought I'd gotten through to you that day, since you said you wanted to drink tea with me again."

Since she'd said she wanted to live.

"And so yesterday, you…"

"Yeah. I believed this peaceful, ordinary year was what you wanted."

Not just Siesta. Nagisa too.

Now that the fighting was over and their missions had been carried out, I'd thought the detectives had finally gotten their happy ending. They'd given me so much. Maybe it was arrogant of me, but I hoped I'd managed to repay them.

"I had the wrong idea, though."

"…Assistant, that's—"

"No, listen. I'm not disparaging myself." I just wanted to acknowledge my own mistake. It was something I'd realized after Nagisa had asked me that question last night.

"Which versions of us did you like?"

It was time to answer that question.

"A minute ago, I said I hated the part of you that doesn't hesitate to sacrifice herself. But…"

I didn't know if I should say this next bit. Everything I'd done had been an attempt to deny this. Holding on to this wish was what had let me move forward and shown me the future. If I said this, I risked overturning all of that. It could put the life I wanted even further out of reach. Even so—

"I thought that ephemeral detective was beautiful, too."

The detective who hadn't hesitated to scatter herself like cherry blossoms, who'd swept away the darkness with a brief flash of light, who'd shone brighter than anyone. I'd loved that radiant detective.

"So this is my apology." This had to be the first time I'd ever genuinely given one to Siesta. "I didn't want to let you die, and I almost sullied the pride of the Ace Detective for the sake of my ego. I'm sorry. Forgive me."

The music was still playing. I drew Siesta closer.

"Did I look cool?" she asked, just a little uneasily. Her face was there in my arms, near my heart.

"Yeah. You were beautiful and cool and dazzling. I think I took your hand that day because the invitation was coming from someone like that."

We'd met in the sky at ten thousand meters. She'd barged into my house and my school, and she'd shown me the solutions to my problems. Then, as she was about to leave on her journey around the world, she'd held out a hand to me, and I'd taken it. I'd had the feeling that going with her would drastically change my life.

"Is that why you said to stay with you as long as you lived, back then?"

Smiling slightly, Siesta dredged up something from seven years ago. At the airport right before she'd left Japan, Siesta had invited me to be her assistant one last time, and my answer had come out like a proposal.

"I seem to recall taking that back."

"Oh, did you? I took it a little seriously and kept you with me for three years."

We grinned at each other.

The music swelled. It was almost time for the dance to end, and for couples to exchange partners.

"All right, Siesta. I'm going to say it again."

Siesta tilted her head slightly.

"Stay with me as long as I live."

Her blue eyes widened.

"Don't ever go away. Not for the rest of your life. Let me stay with you until we die."

I'd seen Siesta leave the world many times before, and those scenes flickered through my mind.

In this moment, I believed the souls of words had power—and I used them to deny those memories.

"No matter what happens, don't disappear. Wherever you're going, take me with you. I'll go anywhere. Whatever unfairness we run into, I'll get through it. And so—"

"I promise." Siesta's radiant eyes gazed at me.

I couldn't hear the music anymore. The only thing I could hear was her voice.

"I'll always take you with me. I'll protect you from unfairness forever. I'll do dumb things with you until we die. And so—"

With a little *thunk*, Siesta let her forehead rest against my chest.

"Make me happy as long as I live."

We stopped dancing. Our breathing was rough, our bodies flushed. Once I'd calmed down a little, I began to hear the voices around me again. The music had ended. Siesta and I were still gazing at each other, but at last, we broke eye contact.

"Did you mean 'as a detective'?"

"You meant 'as an assistant,' didn't you, Kimi?"

Our eyes locked again, and then we both started laughing. Unusually for Siesta, she was laughing so hard she had to wipe away tears, and her smile was the same million-watt one she'd worn on that day.

"Now then, Assistant. What are we going to do next?"

Switching emotional gears entirely, the detective asked her assistant for his decision.

The main show began now.

I drew a deep breath, then gave the answer I hadn't chosen in the other future.

"Siesta, let's begin the maneuver."

◆ March of evil

After the ball, we relocated to the venue where the Ritual of Sacred Return would be held.

It was just before seven. So far, events had played out in roughly the same way as the other future. That was partly because I'd been careful to do the same things, though.

If I changed our environment or what I did too drastically, I wouldn't be able to count on the future I'd seen anymore. I'd been retracing my previous route as closely as I could, making only the changes that were absolutely necessary. This time, again, I did just one thing differently.

"Will these seats do?" Noel asked.

"Yes, here's fine." I nodded, lowering myself into a seat at the front of the hall, on the left side of the first floor. There were only about twenty meters between us and the altar here.

"Sorry to make you reseat us like this."

"No, I understand why you would want to have as clear a view of the ritual as possible. This will be the Tuners' final performance."

...Yeah, that's right. Assuming they manage to complete the ceremony.

"By the way, what happened to Siesta? She's really late," I asked, turning to Nagisa. I hadn't seen Siesta since the ball.

"When girls leave their seats, don't let the reasons concern you."

"Oh, the bathroom, then?"

"Did you abandon your tact by the side of the road?" Nagisa's glare was like an icy knife. What, was I rude?

"It should begin in about five minutes," Noel said, just as she had the first time.

I used that time to get my thoughts in order.

At this point, things were going smoothly. I'd faced the detectives squarely, made sure the Oracle and I were on the same page about the situation, and made my own position firm. However, there were a lot of unknowns from here on out.

During the ritual, someone would probably attempt to snipe Mia again. Why Mia, though? In the previous future, it had happened just as she was about to burn the origin text. They might have attacked so they could steal it.

But that origin text had been a fake. Did the sniper not know? ...No, that wasn't even possible. I'd definitely seen the thing in the crow mask holding a black rifle in the hall. It knew everything. That meant it had sold us out on purpose.

"So they have a goal besides stealing the origin text," I muttered, quietly enough that no one would hear me.

I had no idea if "they" included Stephen and the other Tuners or not. However, the thing in the crow mask that had come from Another Eden was our enemy for sure. The unknown crisis was definitely going to occur. We had to shut it down.

"We're back where we started."

On the day Noel had summoned Siesta and Nagisa, they'd retaken their authority as Tuners; then, on Bruno's request, they had become Ace Detectives again. Now we'd fight the unknown crisis that was going to occur at this ceremony, as they'd originally discussed.

Fate wouldn't change easily, but we could change the way we fought. I was as ready for this as I'd ever be.

"Sorry to keep you waiting." Just then, the latecomer seated herself next to Nagisa.

"You sure took your time, Siesta."

"Yes, I was fixing my makeup. How does it look?" She tilted her head.

"I almost didn't recognize you. You look like a different person."

"That's surprisingly direct."

During our casual exchange, a low bell rang from some untraceable location. And then...

"Let us begin."

At Noel's signal, my second Ritual of Sacred Return began.

The hall's roof retracted, the masked dignitaries appeared, the conch shell sounded, and the kindling was lit. Everything I'd seen the first time was happening again.

Then Mia took the stage. Olivia handed her a sacred text, and she tossed it into the flames, performing her role as the Oracle. White smoke climbed into the sky, and one of the dignitaries who surrounded the platform read a scroll in a foreign tongue. There were other things I needed to focus on right now, though.

"Where is it?" I scanned the hall carefully. The thing in the crow mask had to be here. It was definitely lurking somewhere with that rifle, ready to attack the Oracle.

In the first future, it had been in the seats on the second floor, on the opposite side. As far as I could see from where I was, it wasn't there now. Had it picked up on the fact that I'd concentrated security there?

"...Kimihiko, it's almost time," Nagisa whispered in my ear. Mia would pick up the origin text soon. If something was going to happen, it would be then.

I'd told the two detectives how events were likely to play out. Naturally, they'd been dubious, but they were going along with my plan. I couldn't afford to blow it now.

Before long, the moment came: Olivia handed Mia the origin text. Mia accepted it, then held it out to the blazing flames.

By the time I finally found the thing—in the second-floor seats on the opposite side, just like before—it was already pointing its rifle at Mia.

"! How did it do that?"

I was sure it hadn't been there earlier. The thing in the crow mask had appeared all of a sudden, almost as if it had teleported.

"Mia!" I shouted.

Up on the platform, Mia's eyes narrowed sharply. I'd told her about the attack in advance, too. Yelling her name now wouldn't help her dodge a bullet traveling faster than the speed of sound, though.

"It's all right. If we know the future, we can respond before it happens," said the white-haired girl in the blue gown... Several seconds ago, actually.

By the time I shouted Mia's name, the girl in blue had already lunged for the platform.

The gunshot rang out a second later.

As everyone else covered their eyes or their ears, I kept my eyes fixed on the stage.

Mia had ducked and covered. Standing in front of her, the proxy Ace Detective had swung the musket in her right hand like a sword and knocked the assassin's bullet away.

"Enemy attack!" Bruno Belmondo shouted.

This time, I was able to take a better look at what I hadn't managed to see the first time.

Bruno was sitting on the right-hand side near the front, opposite our group. He pointed at the red-robed figure in the crow mask, but the enemy responded by turning its gun on Bruno.

"Grandfather!" Noel screamed.

The contents of that letter raced through my mind as well. I'd planned for this, though. The White Suit soldiers who were stationed around Bruno fired first, and the thing in the crow mask dropped its rifle. It didn't seem to like its chances against those numbers. It took a superhuman leap back, putting a lot of distance between them.

"Nagisa, do it now."

"I'm on it. Rill's first."

We exchanged nods, then started carrying out our plan. Since we'd been expecting this, our top priority had to be getting people off the battlefield. When I scanned the venue, people had already begun to evacuate on their own, so we helped out. Starting with Rill, who couldn't walk, Nagisa helped the other noncombatants escape.

"Siesta! Get Mia out!" The Oracle was the sniper's target, and we had to make sure she got away as well. I watched the white-haired girl pick up Mia, then head for the exit along with Olivia. That meant we'd protected the origin text, too.

"Now we need to get Bruno out of here…"

When I looked back at the opposite side of the venue, I spotted a dozen White Suits surrounding the thing in the crow mask in an open space on the lower floor. In addition to their guns, the soldiers were leveling heavy weapons and swords in shapes I'd never seen before at the attacker.

For some reason, the thing began to hop lightly.

Boing, boing, boing.

It bounced rhythmically several times, then winked out of sight. A few seconds later, several human heads flew into the air at once. Blood sprayed, dyeing their pure white uniforms red.

How had it beheaded the White Suits? The thing itself was the only one who knew. Then it landed on the floor, and its head turned toward the distant Information Broker.

"Bruno!"

As I shouted, the security team realized that the situation had gone south and rushed over to provide backup. They all fired at once, but the bullets vanished in thin air. This was the same thing crow-mask had done on the cruise. Then the thing made "gun" gestures with both hands.

Bang, bang, bang.

I hadn't heard any real shots. However, every soldier those fingers pointed at collapsed as if they'd actually been shot.

But the soldiers had slowed down the enemy, and the time they'd bought would save the life of the world's wisdom. As Bruno grimaced at the carnage in the hall, he made it through the exit with the help of his guards.

"Noel, we should hurry, too." I grabbed Noel's hand and we made for the nearest exit—but the figure in the crow mask appeared right in front of us. The black mask was right in my face, and my legs locked up. It wasn't just from fear. Before the malice of a superior being, my instincts wouldn't let me move.

"_____"

Its black, hollow eyes told me nothing. Just then, an ally's bullet whizzed between us. With a superhuman acrobatic maneuver, the thing in the crow mask was gone. All it left behind was its bestial smell.

"…! Mr. Kimihiko, this is…" Noel was looking around, wide-eyed.

Maybe I'd let my guard down once that thing was gone. Before I knew it, a group of more than fifty new enemies had invaded the hall.

The men wore gas masks and were dressed all in black, and they carried rifles and machine guns at the ready. Falling into a predetermined formation in the blink of an eye, they surrounded the hall, which still held nearly three hundred people.

"More residents of Another Eden…?"

Naturally, our situation wasn't good. The thing in the crow mask didn't seem to be in the hall anymore, but it had taken out almost all of our armed allies.

I wasn't sure if this was good luck or bad, but as far as I could see, neither Ace Detective was in the hall. That meant they must have gotten away safely with the other hostages. On the other hand, it also meant they weren't going to be able to help me. Mia, Rill, and Bruno were gone as well. The only people left were helpless, normal humans.

"Mr. Kimihiko, we have to do something…"

"It's all right. The enemy doesn't plan to kill us right away, at least."

This formation was meant to keep us from escaping. This was going to become a negotiation.

The next moment, my guess turned out to be right.

The roof closed, and an image appeared on the screen at the front of the hall.

Once again, the being we saw was wearing a crow mask. Was it the one that had just been here, or was this someone else?

I couldn't even tell if it was a man or a woman. In a strange voice that sounded synthesized, it told us the motive behind their attack on justice.

"Federation Government.   Here and now,   you will reveal the secret of the world   which you have hidden."

◆ The masked dolls

They gave us ten minutes to answer. If their demand wasn't met by then, they would kill one hostage.

Once the thing in the crow mask had told us the rules, the screen went dark.

Afterward, those of us who had been left behind were thrown into confusion again.

"…So the enemy really is Another Eden."

The pain of my fingernails digging into my palms made me realize that I'd clenched my fists.

As before, the messenger from Another Eden was demanding the secret of the world. That was the enemy's greatest and only objective. When they told us they'd do nothing if we handed over the origin text, they'd been lying.

Had Stephen tricked me on the other route? Or had he been tricked by the thing in the crow mask? Either way, one thing was clear: Until the Federation Government revealed this "secret of the world," the attacks wouldn't stop. Negotiations and deals no longer meant anything.

"Noel, can I ask one last question?" I spoke to her quietly, below the constant, confused murmuring that filled the hall. "Do you really not have any idea what they're talking about?"

"…I really don't. Those who outrank me may know, but I'm new, and I don't have the authority to learn about such things." Noel shook her head, biting her lip. She wasn't lying. I could tell from her complexion, the movements of her eyes, and the quivering of her voice.

"All right. In that case, I'm going to go ask someone who does know."

"Mr. Kimihiko…?"

I got to my feet, and Noel looked up at me. Watching her out of the corner of my eye, I walked toward the very front of the hall. The Federation Government dignitaries were still there, standing stiff and motionless. Either they hadn't managed to flee in time, or they hadn't intended to run in the first place. I stopped in front of one of them.

Although they were all wearing masks, the shapes and patterns of those masks differed, so it was possible to tell individuals apart. That meant I only had to look to know who this one was.

"Ice Doll, I need to talk to you."

Any of them would have been fine. However, this woman had been particularly involved with me and the Ace Detectives, so she was the one I went to.

"What is this secret of the world that Another Eden wants?"

The masked woman only stood there silently. Every eye in the hall was on us, but none of our enemies tried to interfere. That was fine with me.

"If you people keep pretending you know nothing, one of these hostages will be killed. In fact, since you officials are directly connected to this, the odds that it'll be one of you are good. If you know the answer, hurry up and spill it."

As I reasoned with her, I stayed as calm as I could manage. After a little silence, she spoke. "Ice Doll does not have the authority to answer that question."

The masked woman spoke mechanically, as if what was happening here had nothing to do with her.

"So it's just that you don't have the authority to answer, not that you don't know?"

"Ice Doll does not have the authority to answer that question."

"…People have died during the global crises before now. If you let Another Eden invade, the disasters will begin again."

I wasn't insisting that they accept all of Another Eden's demands, but so far, the Federation Government's policy had been to delay without a plan. This unprecedented disaster was all that lay ahead of us. The world already had one foot in the door to that hell.

"Isn't it the Tuners' mission to head off those disasters?"

For the first time, Ice Doll said something that wasn't a canned phrase. "...Yeah, it is."

They didn't need Ice Doll and the rest to give them orders. The Tuners' missions were determined by their own free will. By their desire to save people. That was why my Ace Detectives had been peerlessly beautiful from moment to moment as they risked their lives. They weren't wrong.

"But you people just sit back on your thrones, so you don't have the right to say that."

Every time a disaster broke out, they assembled the Tuners and made them fight, either until the storm had passed or a Tuner lost their life. The Federation Government had devoured the lives of heroes for the sake of a temporary peace.

They sat on their thrones, back where it was safe, while the Tuners bled. The Tuners would work themselves to the bone and die in battle, and then their shields of justice vanished without even leaving names behind.

"Do you remember how their backs looked?"

Ice Doll didn't answer.

"Where were you on the day the Ace Detective carried out her mission at the cost of her life? The day the Magical Girl accepted that she'd never be able to walk again? Tell me, where were you? When the Vampire ended the way he did, where were you watching from?"

I knew the masked official wouldn't answer those questions.

I wasn't saying these things so someone would hear. It didn't matter if they didn't resonate with anybody. I just put that unfairness into words and got them out.

"Ice Doll doesn't have the authority to answer that question."

By now, it didn't even make me mad. I'd left anger behind long ago.

What I was about to say had to do with the future.

"Ice Doll— No, Federation Government. Don't think your way of doing things is going to work forever. One of these days, all your allies will desert you. As a matter of fact, I already know a few who are leaning that way."

For example, the former Inventor, the former Revolutionary, and the former Hero were all about to abandon the Federation Government. The surge of rebellion was already building.

Besides...

"The detectives and I know *the truth about the Mizoev Federation*, which forms the nucleus of the Federation Government. If we spread that around, we can turn the world upside down whenever we want."

The truth we'd identified probably rivaled "the secret of the world," whatever that was. At this point, the power dynamic between us and the Federation Government wasn't one-sided by any means. We had our guns trained on each other at all times.

"You can't stay complacent and claim not to have authority forever. Before long, you'll take off those masks voluntarily and start talking. You'll beg the detectives to save the world."

Even after that, Ice Doll didn't take off her mask.

Fine. At least for now, I'll respect your stance.

I checked my watch. We were out of time.

"Disappear as a voiceless doll."

In the next instant, right in front of me, Ice Doll's head flew off.

One of the men in gas masks had done it. Ten minutes into the incident, Ice Doll was the first hostage killed.

"...A doll?" someone murmured.

After a short delay, Ice Doll's body toppled over.

Her severed head rolled across the ground nearby. However, there was no blood. All that was there was what I'd begun to anticipate partway through that conversation: a ruined doll.

"Are the other government officials the same?"

Even before the ceremony had begun, these people had been replaced by dolls.

No doubt the real people under the masks were watching all of this play out remotely. They'd evacuated somewhere safe and left the Tuners to handle the cleanup.

"What a farce."

I hadn't managed to get that vital answer out of her, though.

All my strength drained away, and I sank into a nearby seat.

"Mr. Kimihiko..." Noel had come up to me, and now she reached out, sounding worried. However, before she could rub my back, she seemed to realize something and retracted her hand.

"Let us move to the next phase."

I heard the voice of the thing in the crow mask, although I couldn't tell where it was coming from. Once again, an image appeared on the screen. This time, there were several hundred men and women in swallowtail coats and gowns. They were standing in the venue where the ball had been held.

Every one of those people looked nervous. Just like us, they were being held captive by men in gas masks.

"…! Grandfather…!"

Noel had spotted Bruno in that image. Nagisa was beside him. In that case, had the Men in Black stationed at the palace been neutralized by the messenger's group, too?

"Even Miss Siesta…," Noel murmured.

As far as I could see, the detective didn't have her musket. Fighting all those armed enemies with nothing but her bare hands would be tough. And the sheer number of hostages made the situation a whole lot worse.

"Next   we will blow up   this hall."

After announcing what would happen in another ten minutes, the enemy cut the picture again.

This time, it wouldn't be just a single government official. Unless we exposed the secret of the world, everyone in that hall would die. The Ace Detectives, the Oracle, the Magical Girl, the Information Broker—everybody.

"We've got no time to lose."

This would probably be the only chance I'd get to play my remaining card.

The girl beside me was staring at the ground. I spoke to her without turning to look. "I knew it. The view from the train that's carrying a bomb isn't a pretty one, Noel."

◇ Pandora's box and the world's taboo

"Next   we will blow up   this hall."

The enemy's eerie voice echoed throughout the venue.

This statement set the large room buzzing, but the surrounding group in gas masks leveled their machine guns at us until we fell silent again.

Fifteen minutes ago, a sniper had attacked the Oracle during the Ritual of Sacred Return. Most of the people attending the ceremony had run for it, but men in gas masks who'd been stationed throughout the palace had rounded us up and herded us into this hall. We were still there, under orders not to move, completely hostage to the terrorists.

I wasn't near Mia, Rill, or Siesta. Kimihiko was probably still in the hall where the ceremony had been held. I had to do my part here. And so—

"I'm glad you were close to me, Bruno," I said to the old gentleman beside me, softly enough that the men in gas masks wouldn't hear.

"No, I'm the one who feels safer here, young Miss Ace Detective." Bruno's white whiskers shifted as he grinned. His all-encompassing generosity soothed my nerves just a little.

"I'm sorry," he went on gently. "I knew someone might be targeting me, yet my sense of duty kept me from backing out of the ceremony. I was unable to come up with any countermeasures, and now we've fallen into the enemy's hands. It's really deplorable."

"Please don't apologize. If you're going to put it that way, Siesta and I are the Ace Detectives, and we couldn't head off this crisis, either. We're all responsible."

This wasn't anybody's fault.

We were all trying to do the right thing. Even now, we were struggling to get there. That was what this was about.

For the sake of doing my own version of "the right thing," I asked Bruno a question. "So, Bruno. How much do you really know about Another Eden, or about the secret the Federation Government is hiding?"

I swallowed hard, and there was a moment of silence.

Had Bruno been defeated by the enemy? Had he failed to do anything at all? He was the world's wisdom itself; did he really have no idea who the enemy actually was, or what secret the world held? That wasn't possible.

If there was a reason he was staying here quietly anyway, it must have been that...

"Can you really not answer that? If it's information that could destroy the balance of the world..."

Bruno Belmondo, the Information Broker, possessed knowledge that could be more of a threat than any weapon, and he never shared it with others.

He was no longer a Tuner, but he still lived by that philosophy, even under these circumstances—no, because of these circumstances. The Information Broker worked constantly to keep the scales balanced.

"Bruno, please. The things you know could save lives."

If Bruno Belmondo was still captive to the Tuner way of life, then I would be, too. One more time, as the Ace Detective, I'd talk the Information Broker around. Besides... "Weren't you hoping we'd get it out of you anyway?"

Bruno himself was the one who'd first tried to make me the Ace Detective again. Two weeks ago, when he'd visited the detective agency and told us he wanted us to return to the position of Ace Detective, he'd said that what he could do alone was limited, and he was trying to acquire more comrades.

"Once, there was a detective girl who asked me for a favor," Bruno said, sounding somehow nostalgic. "In this world, there's something known as an absolute taboo. A Pandora's box that must not be opened. A sealed coffin that will unleash disaster on the world. However, there was a time when I was desperate to learn about it. As the Information Broker who embodied the world's wisdom, I felt I had no choice," he went on. "One day, someone with the same ambition appeared. As the Information Broker, I was merely a database, but he was someone who used that information to act—"

"—The Ace Detective?" I asked.

Bruno nodded wordlessly.

This interaction was how the roles of the Information Broker and the Ace Detective played out.

We'd tackled our missions together that way since time immemorial.

"However, he forced Pandora's box open, came into contact with the world's taboo, and died."

When Bruno said "he," he meant the former Ace Detective. The one who'd come before Siesta and me.

"And he told you about that taboo? About the answer?"

Bruno didn't answer that question, either. This time, maybe even the Information Broker really didn't know.

"The one thing I can say is that Pandora's box still slumbers somewhere in the world."

"Is what's inside it the secret the messenger from Another Eden wants? Does the Federation Government have custody of it?"

Bruno started to answer, but just then—

A man in a gas mask pushed the muzzle of a gun against his back.

"Bruno…!"

I was startled, but Bruno only held up his hands, demonstrating that he didn't plan to resist. Then he grinned and asked the man, "Did you need me for something?"

The world's wisdom is about to perish.

The letter that had been sent to our agency flitted through my mind.

Then the man in the gas mask marched Bruno away at gunpoint.

"It's all right." As he left, Bruno smiled at me. "In every era, I believe in the Ace Detective."

◆ The one thing we wanted to know

The view from the train that's carrying a bomb isn't a pretty one.

Noel didn't pretend she didn't know what I meant. She only pressed her lips together tightly, as if she'd been expecting this.

"You knew this was going to happen, didn't you, Noel?"

"Yes. After all, we'd been warned that the messenger from Another Eden would attack. I also knew Grandfather might be caught up in it."

That was true. Roughly two weeks ago, Noel and Bruno had alerted us to the crisis that could happen at the Ritual of Sacred Return. But…

"After that, we got a letter saying, 'The world's wisdom is about to perish.' You sent that, didn't you?"

Silence fell between us.

The hall was as noisy as ever, and I heard quite a few people denouncing the absent Federation Government officials. Nobody was listening in on our conversation.

"That sounds as if it was written by a criminal. Why do you feel I'd send a letter like that to the Shirogane Detective Agency, Mr. Kimihiko?"

"Suspecting someone who's been watching you the whole time is a pretty natural reaction, isn't it?"

"………"

My retort was blunt, but Noel's expression didn't flicker. That didn't mean she was admitting to anything, though.

"Noel, you've been watching us constantly since yesterday. You came to the airport to get me, you invited us on that cruise, and you kept tabs on our movements after that."

"You were invited to the ceremony. As a member of the Federation Government, it was my job to attend you."

"Rill and Mia told me nobody from the government attended them. When you contacted us, you had a reason of your own."

"…As I told you, I wanted your advice regarding the threat to Grandfather."

"Yeah, speaking of Bruno. Yesterday evening, he and I met up, just the two of us. *Who did you hear about that from?*"

In the car today, on the way to the venue, Noel had started out by asking me if I'd slept well yesterday, and in the course of that conversation, she'd said: "You met Grandfather again, didn't you?"

I hadn't told Noel about that. She shouldn't have had that information. She couldn't have gotten it without watching me or eavesdropping on us.

"I heard about it from Grandfather yesterday. He said he'd talked with you."

"Impossible. There's no way the Information Broker would have broken a promise and leaked information that easily."

Bruno wouldn't slip up like that, not even with his granddaughter. I'd set that meeting up in secret. I'd specifically told him it might be harder to talk if Noel was there. There was no way he hadn't understood me.

"Noel. Look at this."

That was when I got a text with an image attached, and the timing could not have been better.

"It's a photo of a bug. They found it in our hotel room."

Of course, Noel had arranged for us to stay in that room. I could only think of one reason it would have a listening device in it.

"...Why now?"

"We would have preferred to look for it ourselves, but the room might have had hidden cameras, too. We couldn't afford to search for bugs like that; it would've looked too sketchy."

We'd finally managed to get proof, though: A certain idol had found this for us, using her impressive insight. I'd go along with all of her whims for as long as she wanted later. I was so glad that her overseas performance tomorrow was right here in France.

"Also, this. There was a miniature bug in the coat I wore last night." I showed Noel the follow-up image Saikawa had sent. "That one was packed in my suitcase. They must have messed with it at the airport, huh?"

That was why my luggage had been so late: because the trap was already being set.

"...You picked up on that, and you still wore the coat?"

"I only thought it was a possibility. When I was talking with Nagisa in the park last night, though, I intentionally brought up Bruno. That's how you knew, isn't it?"

Ever since Siesta, Nagisa, and I had arrived in France— Actually, from the moment we'd boarded our flight, we'd suspected we might be under surveillance. For that reason, I'd regularly laid traps for Noel in our conversations, and when the detectives and I held strategy meetings at the hotel, we'd conversed entirely by text, acting as if we were just messing around with our smartphones.

"But this doesn't hold together logically. You haven't said what initially made you suspect I would watch you at all."

"You weren't the only one we suspected."

Noel gulped, gazing into my face.

"We don't trust anybody. Even as we banter and laugh together, we constantly doubt what's happening right in front of us, investigate it minutely, and weigh it. That's a detective's job. It's how we do things."

There was a time when we'd thought that if the other option was doubting people, we'd rather just get tricked—Nagisa in particular. However, in the midst of all our cases and battles, we'd learned that that alone wouldn't let us save people. Pure hearts weren't what we needed.

So now, this was how I thought: If the other option was believing people, it was better to trick them. When we wanted to save many things at once, we became scam artists as well as detectives.

"Noel, be honest. Tell me what you're hiding."

I'd played all my cards now. This was the only objective proof we had; Siesta had been the one to suggest it. Hopefully, it would be enough to make Noel fold.

"Not yet." Noel shook her head slightly. "I admit I had you under surveillance. But that doesn't mean I sent that letter. Mr. Kimihiko, what makes you so certain I'm involved?"

…Right. After providing proof, we needed to demonstrate a motive. This time, I'd borrow Nagisa's ability. Her words had power, and I was sure she'd argue Noel down. "Sorry we weren't able to take your request."

Noel's eyes widened.

"You thought if you told us 'The world's wisdom is about to perish,' the Ace Detectives would take action to protect Bruno, didn't you?"

That hadn't been advance warning of a crime. It had been a request for the detectives to take a case. Noel had wanted us to protect the world's wisdom from the hands of the enemy. She could have just asked us to protect Bruno directly, but she'd probably assumed her appeal would be more efficient if the situation seemed worse than it actually was.

"You also guessed that the detectives were bound to *thoroughly investigate Bruno Belmondo, the person they were supposed to guard.* That was what you were really after."

That was exactly right: Noel had sent us that letter because she'd wanted the detectives to investigate something about Bruno.

"I don't need to turn to a detective to learn about Grandfather. I know everything there is to—"

"No. There's something even you don't know about him."

It was a question Noel had always kept locked away in the depths of her heart, but she'd finally touched that black box.

"You wanted to know why Bruno Belmondo adopted you, and why he dissolved your relationship after more than ten years."

Noel looked down. Her long gray hair fell like a screen to hide her face.

From this point on, there was a chance that my subjective opinions would get mixed in with the facts. But I wanted her to hear this as a hypothesis. "Noel. Roughly two weeks ago, you learned that Another Eden was trying to disclose a secret that the Federation Government was protecting."

Noel had probably picked up on the fact that they were holding on to top secret information long ago, though. She'd told me yesterday that there were rumors about it.

"That was when you hit on a plan. You'd use this situation to learn about that secret."

"Whatever for? I inherited this position out of necessity, and I have no personal interest in secrets like that."

She probably did mean that. I had never gotten the impression she took pride in fulfilling her duties as a government official, or in having returned to the noble Lupwise family.

On the other hand, she had another emotion that was very hard for her to fight.

"I doubt you can say that even Bruno doesn't matter, though."

She squeezed her eyes shut.

"You've always had doubts about your monthly dinners with him. Why does he still meet with you, even though he isn't fostering you anymore? Does he have some other reason? For example—*trying to get information on the secret of the world out of you?*"

Noel had guessed that the Belmondo and Lupwise families were bound to each other by that secret, and that it might have been why Bruno had adopted her. Since she had the potential to become a government official someday, he might have been attempting to get closer to the world's secret by buying her affection.

Noel was the child of a mistress, and her family had treated her coldly. If Bruno had said he wanted to adopt her, the Lupwises would have had no reason to refuse.

In addition, Bruno had somehow known that the Lupwise family heir would vanish in the near future. As a result, the position of government official would go to Noel, putting her closer to the world's secret.

"...Are you implying that I always doubted Grandfather's love?"

I was. A girl had suddenly experienced love for the first time in her life, and she'd wanted to know why. She'd feared there might be some ulterior motive behind it. That was why, right now...

"You used this convenient crisis. You thought if you could disclose the world's secret, you'd be able to learn what Bruno really wanted."

"That...isn't... I didn't want this, at least. That's why I—!" Noel was keeping her voice down, but her fervent emotions came through loud and clear.

Gently, I squeezed her hand. "Yeah, so I'd like to apologize to you. You did want to resolve this sooner, didn't you? After all, you kept asking us—well, the detectives—to help you. You wanted us to investigate Bruno and protect him."

Noel flinched.

"I'm sorry we couldn't help you."

As far as Noel was concerned, she'd sown the seeds well in advance, and yet we hadn't gotten any of the results she'd wanted. It must have been really irritating. Even keeping us under surveillance after we arrived in France hadn't gotten her the information she wanted.

Today, she'd reluctantly resorted to entrusting her long-cherished wish to the mastermind.

"Noel, please, help me. I promise we'll grant your wish later. I want you to tell me anything else you know. You've figured out what's really going on here, haven't you?"

We still hadn't learned what the hidden secret was, or anything about Another Eden's messengers. The origin text hadn't shown me those answers.

As a matter of fact, we'd hoped to find out the truth by keeping an eye on Noel. But she'd kept that information hidden, even after our failure to do what she wanted. What she'd gone that far to protect was—

"You win. I'll tell you everything." Noel's voice was slightly tearful. "I know who really orchestrated this crisis."

Just then, the door at the front of the hall flew open with a loud *bang*, and two figures entered. One was an armed man in a gas mask. He was holding his gun to an elderly man's back.

"…Bruno?"

As the two of them slowly climbed the steps to the stage, the Information Broker's expression was tense. At the altar, they both turned to face forward.

"I thought I gave you enough time, but no one has come forward with the answer."

It wasn't the man in the gas mask who spoke. That man had already lowered his gun and was waiting off to the side.

"Please, Mr. Kimihiko," Noel begged in a trembling voice. "Stop Grandfather."

Bruno Belmondo, Information Broker and the world's wisdom, *took out a pistol and shot a nearby government official doll.*

"Don't you think it's time humanity awoke from this transient peace?"

◆ Rebellious tuning

All the men in gas masks bowed in perfect sync to Bruno Belmondo, who stood in the center of the stage. By now, it was patently clear who was in control.

"…I had a feeling you were behind this."

When we'd realized Noel had been the one to send us that second wish—"I want you to protect the world's wisdom"—we'd also realized it was possible that Bruno was the mastermind.

Basically, maybe Noel wasn't asking us to keep Bruno from becoming a victim, but rather to keep him from doing harm. We just hadn't wanted to believe it.

The hall was still buzzing over the entrance of this entirely unexpected mastermind. I was the only one who got to my feet.

The closest enemy took aim at me, but at Bruno's signal, he lowered his weapon. Apparently the Information Broker was willing to talk with me.

"Bruno Belmondo. Who are you?"

There were no detectives here. It was my job to ask the questions.

"What are your ties to Another Eden? What are you hoping to accomplish by committing terrorism?"

The crow-mask and the gas-masks had to be residents of Another Eden. If Bruno Belmondo was leading them, who was he?

But I didn't expect Bruno's answer.

"We do not belong to Eden."

He claimed that *no one* here had any connection to Another Eden.

"What? Don't tell me you made the place up entirely."

No, that couldn't be. The Federation Government had said that Another Eden had been making contact with them since time immemorial. Siesta had mentioned hearing that story as well.

"Another Eden does exist. Somewhere in this world, or perhaps somewhere in space. On this occasion, we simply imitated them."

"So you were just impersonating them? Why would you do that?"

"I believe we've already explained our objective to you, many times over."

...Yeah, they had. They—or at least Bruno—wanted to learn the identity of something the Federation Government was hiding, then steal it.

"Is that why you approached the Lupwise family ten years ago? For their strong ties to the Federation Government?"

He'd adopted the five-year-old Noel because he'd foreseen that she would be a government official someday, and that this would bring him closer to the world's secret.

"A solid deduction." Bruno looked down at me from the stage, stroking his beard. Then his eyes went to Noel, who was sitting beside me. "I waited a long time for that girl to approach the core of the world. Three years ago, the time came. The head of the Lupwise family passed away suddenly, and his heir vanished. As I'd anticipated, the girl inherited the family's seat in the Federation Government. However..." Bruno's eyes grew disappointed. "After that, my plans went awry. She was only a makeshift successor, and she showed no sign of being allowed near the core. I waited two years, but that time was wasted."

Noel hung her head. Her shoulders seemed to be trembling. "And so you gave up on me a year ago, Grandfather, and…"

No matter how little I wanted to, I knew what the rest of that sentence would be. Bruno's hopes hadn't played out, so he'd dissolved his relationship with Noel. If she'd never be in a position to learn the world's secret, then he had no use for her.

"A year later, then, I decided to implement this plan. At the Ritual of Sacred Return, where many people near the world's core would assemble, I would ask the identity and location of the world's secret. However, no one here seems to know the answer, either."

Bruno's disappointed gaze traveled around the hall again. He'd gathered and threatened Federation Government personnel, former Tuners, and international VIPs, but in the end, no one had been able to give him what he wanted.

"It wasn't entirely in vain, though. The masked dignitaries fled, using dolls as decoys. They do know the answer. Therefore, we will advance," Bruno said, as if he were declaring war on the world.

"You're going to find Ice Doll and the others? And you're going to keep up the terrorism until you get what you want? It won't work. Now that you've gone this far, the Federation Government is going to view you as an enemy of the world. The world won't let Bruno Belmondo get away."

At the very least, the Ace Detectives would capture him.

His ambition would never be realized.

"I don't need to be the one who reaches the answer." As Bruno spoke, he was gazing into the distance. "It's enough if someone—anyone—does it. As long as the world remembers, that's enough. Even if I fall here, the wave of rebellion has begun, and it won't stop."

Bruno was echoing the argument I'd made to the Federation Government. I'd told them that, while they sat on their thrones way back where it was safe, a spirit of rebellion was building. That the Inventor and the Revolutionary and the Hero were already on the verge of abandoning them.

"…I see. So Stephen's group were all your comrades, too?"

They really had tricked me, in that other future. The thing in the crow mask, Stephen, and Bruno all wanted the same thing. Their attempt to steal the origin text and their attack on the Ritual of Sacred Return had both been part of a revolt against the organization and order of the Federation Government. But then… "What drove you that far? Why would you do all that to rebel against the Federation Government?"

I resented Ice Doll and the other members of the government, too. I could understand feeling intolerable anger toward them. However, Bruno's claim had a different sort of heat to it.

"Is it because you want to know this secret they've got? This can't be your thirst for information as the former Information Broker. What's the point?"

He'd already retired from his position as the Information Broker. What was the secret he wanted to know badly enough to drag all these people into danger? What was Bruno Belmondo's desire? What could he want so intensely that he'd become an enemy of the world, sacrificing everything—

"You're still pretending you don't know?"

Bruno's reaction wasn't what I'd expected.

He looked more angry than suspicious. It was as if he thought I was trying to misdirect him or give intentionally evasive answers.

"Why does no one know? Why doesn't anyone remember? Why has the world forgotten these words? What other 'secret of the world' could there possibly be?"

Bruno's eyes flew open, and his hand tightened on his gun.

"It's what the Federation Government has kept hidden. What even I, the Information Broker, haven't managed to reach. The world's taboo—the Akashic records!"

Complete silence fell in the hall.

Everyone listened until Bruno stopped speaking, then considered his words.

The time it took for me to say anything felt like an eternity. That was probably inevitable, though.

"What the hell are the Akashic records?"

The term was genuinely unfamiliar to me. Noel also shook her head.

Technically, though, I did have a vague grasp of the concept.

If I recalled, it was the memory of the world itself, recorded since Earth—or possibly the universe—began. I couldn't visualize it in any concrete way, though.

"You're saying you did all this so you could find out what these Akashic records are?" I asked, watching Bruno's face. I didn't understand what he meant.

Bruno wasn't disgusted. He wasn't surprised. The emotion in his face was despair.

"Let me ask you again." Eyes still wide, Bruno doubled down on his question. "The Tuners are the shields who defend the world. How many of them are there?"

"Eleven...right?"

"Then have you ever heard the term 'the Singularity'?"

"...? Isn't that some kind of math term?"

"I see. That's enough."

Bruno lowered his gun. He wasn't looking at me anymore.

"This really is as far as this world goes."

Then what were his keen eyes fixed on now? The question suddenly scared me.

"As you say, I'll be punished soon. In that case, I'll carry out my final mission here."

After a short silence, Bruno's eyes turned to me again. "The following is a warning."

In the next instant, a new image flashed onto the screen.

The screen was split into sixteen sections. In each section, a world leader was being held at knife- or gunpoint by someone in a gas mask.

"This world is not peaceful. The crises are still very much with us. Even so, humanity persists in the naive belief that peace will continue. Therefore, I make this declaration to the entire human race."

That's right; he'd said this was a warning.

"I am about to tune this world, as Evil."

◆ The will that seeks justice is...

In the next instant, all the gas-masked men in the hall leveled their guns at us at once.

"...Bruno. What the hell are you thinking?"

Bruno had originally caused this incident to learn the world's hidden secret, but no sooner had he seen that his wish wouldn't be granted than he'd shifted to blatant terrorism. If he'd had all those agents in position around the world already, had he predicted this would happen? Either way, what he was trying to do now was...

"Do you really intend to become an enemy of the world?"

As a Tuner, Bruno Belmondo's top priority had been preserving the balance of the world. Whenever the world was about to fall into the hands of some great evil, he'd always protected it as a hero. However, he'd just announced that he would tune this world as Evil.

"Evil doesn't necessarily come from outside the world." He gestured to the left side of his chest with his pistol. "Evil is always in here."

I felt as if someone else had told me something similar, long ago.

He'd been an enemy. A man I'd once fought with the detective.

—A man? Who?

"Let me ask you this. Is the world really peaceful?"

The next thing I knew, the screen showed an image of a vast, burning forest. Had it been taken from a movie, or was it a past natural disaster? The image shifted to a slum. A small, painfully skinny girl was rummaging through a pile of garbage that spilled out into the street, searching for food.

"These are crises that are happening to our neighbors at this very moment."

The image on the screen changed again. The sound of tanks firing played. In a war zone, soldiers were putting their lives on the line. These weren't movies, nor were they footage from the past. This was really happening somewhere in the world, right now.

"Compared to the disasters we Tuners dealt with, perhaps these aren't serious enough to be called 'global crises.' However, at the very least,

I wouldn't call this peace. These sparks are still smoldering, and one day, they will create a genuine global crisis."

He was right. When it came to disasters, there was no "big" or "small." Even now, there were calamities and battles happening in our world.

Stephen had said he was still working to save the wounded in war zones. The story Charlie had told me, that anecdote from her past, might actually have been recent. Then there was the question Hel had asked me: Were there really no crying girls in the world anymore?

Bruno Belmondo, the man who knew the world, was giving us a warning.

"We put our faith in a transient peace and surrendered our powers. In the near future, a real disaster will strike again. When it does, we will suffer defeat."

That was why Bruno was voluntarily choosing evil.

He had been a symbol of justice. By becoming a great evil in the eyes of the world, he would maintain balance. He would tune it.

Humanity had soaked for too long in a tepid peace—he wouldn't let them forget the existence of evil.

"Is that why your group tried to shut down this ceremony of peace?"

If the Ritual of Sacred Return had been completed, the Tuners would have been gone, even though we'd need them to fight the disaster. That was why Bruno and his people had attacked the ceremony and tried to steal the origin text. He hadn't genuinely wanted the origin text itself. His goal had been to force the ritual to fail and keep the Tuners tied to their missions.

"You're saying you don't mind defying justice for the sake of your goal?"

"Only justice that runs counter to our ideals."

…So in the end, it came back to that, huh? Flawless justice and transient peace. Bruno believed in the former, while Mia and I had tried to rely on the latter. In order to make his unblemished justice a reality, he was barring our way as Evil.

"Those who have special powers should use those powers for the good of the world. It isn't a right. It's a duty."

"You're telling the Tuners to keep carrying out their missions until they die?"

"Yes. On that point alone, I'm in agreement with the Federation Government."

Then, from this stage of justice, Bruno urged on his comrades around the world. "Rise up. Take up your swords, level your guns. Defeat evil, destroy me. Carry out justice until your lives run out."

—He wasn't wrong about any of this.

I sincerely thought that, as a Tuner, Bruno wasn't wrong.

It wasn't that his speech had convinced me. I'd been familiar with that mindset for years. Someone close to me had given me a thorough education in the philosophy of justice.

Siesta.

Like Bruno, she'd been one of the shields of justice, and she'd been saying things like that since I met her. She'd said it was in her DNA to save people. Siesta had said she was born to be the Ace Detective. I was sure that was correct. For a Tuner who guarded the world, that was probably the ideal.

Even so…

"Why does making a peaceful world require sacrifices to justice?"

Why was it always Siesta? Why always Nagisa? Why were the people who tried to stay true to justice the only ones who got unhappy endings? That was why I'd done that day over. I'd tried to overturn the future the sacred texts had determined. Even if it meant denying the Ace Detective's justice, I'd looked for a different route.

It was the same now. If there was a way to save the detectives, I'd use the origin text or whatever it took and do this over as often as I had to. I wasn't asking for much. I just wanted an ordinary life where those two could drink tea and eat apple pie in peace.

"Bruno. Don't you think trying to satisfy your messiah complex with the feeling you've saved the world is basically abandoning justice entirely?"

The sort of peace that was built on one person's heroic sacrifice didn't need to be glorified anywhere except picture books.

"Will you keep soaking in this transient world, then? You're welcome to do so," Bruno murmured. His eyes were still filled with disappointment. "As long as you can stop evil with a false justice like that."

He put down his pistol. In exchange, he brought out—a red switch.

Everyone in the hall knew what that meant.

"Grandfather! Please don't!" Noel's face was anguished.

The screen showed the hall where the ball had been held. There were several hundred hostages inside. Bruno was about to detonate the bomb he'd rigged up there.

"Those who've refused to see an unbearable reality have no right to dream of happiness," Bruno said. His eyes were wide, his voice filled with passion. His finger reached for the switch.

"Yeah, you're right," I told him. "I was wrong."

Bruno hesitated.

I knew what my mistake had been. I'd tried to make Siesta and Nagisa graduate from being Tuners to satisfy my own ego. The result of that had been that first future. I was only their assistant; I didn't have the right to do that.

"Not getting things wrong is tough."

This was no place for self-mockery. I just let it sink in, as simple fact. Sometimes not getting things wrong was harder than doing what was right. That was true for everybody, though.

Mia, Noel, Bruno... All of them had secrets, and they'd all made choices before heading into this ceremony. All of them had been correct, and they'd all been mistaken.

Still, there was one thing I knew for sure.

Even now, there was just one thing I could believe in.

I used it to answer the question Bruno had posed.

"If both you and I got it wrong, then let's have the detectives set us straight."

After all, that was what the world's wisdom had wanted last night.

"Bruno. I still don't think your justice was a total mistake."

The voice spoke from above us. When I looked up, I saw a sky full of stars. The roof of the hall had been opened again.

The voice's owner—the white-haired Ace Detective—touched down in front of me, facing away.

"Why are you here...?" Bruno murmured in a daze, as if he were dreaming.

It was no wonder he was surprised, or that he'd gotten careless. After all, the white-haired Ace Detective was visible in the image of the hall on the screen.

"You didn't notice? Between the ball and the ritual, *the detective and the maid who has her face switched places.*"

The maid had escaped from this hall, but the real detective had stayed, watching the situation unfold from her hiding place. She'd laid her plans carefully to bring all this to an end.

"Noches. I'm borrowing what you left here."

As Siesta broke into a run, I reached under the seats and grabbed what the white-haired maid had left us. And then—

"Siesta! Catch!"

As Siesta ran, I threw the musket to her with all my might.

"So this was the right move."

No—I'd hesitated just a little.

But Siesta, that gun really does suit you.

The detective who brushed happy dreams aside, who threw her peaceful life away, who lived from moment to moment like the wind—she was more noble than anyone, more fragile, and...more beautiful. And so...

"Siesta, you should be the Ace Detective again."

Siesta caught the gun and pointed it straight ahead. "Brilliant work, Assistant."

Just now, I'd finally managed to choose a future.

"————!" Bruno's face twisted slightly.

The bullet Siesta fired knocked the switch out of his hand.

"...I see, Ace Detective. So you'll dance the waltz of death with me?"

Siesta had leaped onto the stage, and Bruno held out his right hand to her.

"Bruno?" Siesta frowned, as if she couldn't read the intent behind his smile. Then it hit her. "Don't let them press the switch!" she shouted, turning back.

If she meant the bombs rigged to the venue, she'd already—

—Oh. No, that wasn't it. She meant *the bomb capsule implanted in Bruno himself.*

Siesta had told me about it, a long time ago. A bomb had been embedded in the Information Broker's body in order to protect what he knew, in case he was captured and tortured by a hostile organization. The switch was entrusted to someone else. And the ones who held that switch were—

"...I get it! *All these men in gas masks are former Men in Black, huh?!*"

They were Bruno's comrades, former fellow Tuners who still followed his principles.

Every one of the men in the hall took a red switch out of his jacket. Bruno's life wasn't in the hands of just one person: the Men in Black were an organization. No matter what we did, we'd never be able to take all the detonator switches out of all of those hands at once.

Bruno Belmondo was preparing to lay down his life, as Evil.

"Siesta, run!"

That meant all I could do was try to get her out of there.

But—

"Why? Why would you do that?"

The perplexed, trembling voice belonged to Bruno himself.

I couldn't blame him. Every Man in Black in the room had lowered his switch.

"I see. They won't take an order that would make you die like this." Siesta lowered her gun as well.

"Impossible." Bruno wasn't flustered now. He shook his head, denying what was happening. "Prioritizing their emotions over their mission? The proud members of the Men in Black would never..."

"It isn't that strange," Siesta said, and Bruno raised his head. "After all, we Tuners are human."

Just then, there was a loud noise behind us.

A riot squad had kicked the door open and rushed in to provide backup. At that, everyone in the hall scrambled for the exit. Nobody stopped them.

"Oh, I see. Did that girl put you up to this?" As he realized what must have happened, Bruno's eyes narrowed.

"I'm not a big fan of the way you put that." Nagisa Natsunagi, the situation's second key player, walked toward us. "It's simple, though. No one wanted you to die as a villain."

As Nagisa came closer, she took off her earpiece. Had she been using that to talk to the Men in Black? Had she asked them whether they were really okay with letting the hero who'd been a Tuner longer than anyone else die as someone evil?

"Two weeks ago, when I picked up the Ace Detective's musket from the Men in Black, one of them made a formal request. He asked me to protect the Information Broker."

Nagisa had already formed a pact with some of the Men in Black. She'd told me so yesterday, during the stealth strategy-meeting-by-text we'd had at the hotel.

However, she'd said the Men in Black hadn't told her the whole truth two weeks ago, either. She hadn't known that Bruno was the mastermind behind these incidents. All the Men in Black had told her was that they wanted her to protect the Information Broker, and that they would assist her. At the very last minute, the Men in Black had also been trying to balance the scales of justice.

Nagisa had picked up on their intentions during the ceremony today and worked to save Bruno.

"You could never be a villain, Grandfather." One other person had believed in Nagisa's passion: a girl who'd spent longer with Bruno than anyone else. His faded eyes fell to where she stood below the stage. "The right hand of Evil isn't that soft. Your hands are for saving and guiding the weak."

Noel reached for his hand, which she'd probably held countless times. She was remembering the warmth of her kind teacher.

"It's as you said—everyone's heart has evil in it." Nagisa had reached us, and as she spoke to Bruno, she rubbed Noel's shoulders. "As long as evil is rampant in us, wars will occur. Disasters will break out. Someday, an enormous crisis is bound to strike this world. It will hit when everyone's come to take peace for granted. I understand that." Nagisa bit her lip.

"If you understand, then why?" Bruno had been stubbornly silent, but now he started to speak. "The world has no messengers of justice now.

When we're struck with an irreparable disaster one day, there will be no one to save us. That's why I—"

Nagisa shook her head, climbing the steps to the stage. "Even if we don't have our titles as Tuners, we seek justice, and our wills will never die." Siesta came to stand beside Nagisa, gently nestling close to her. "It's all right. There are two detectives here. Just watch; we'll save the world twice over."

Bruno smiled, sending wrinkles across his cheeks.

"*Corretto.* Good answer."

And the hero crumpled to the floor like a dead man.

◆ To the you and me who know nothing

A few hours after that, late at night, Bruno Belmondo summoned me.

In a room in the palace where the ball and the ceremony had taken place, the elderly hero lay on a bed, his face haggard.

"I'm sorry. I know you must be tired," he said, the moment he saw me. It made the previous battle between us seem unreal.

"I couldn't sleep anyway," I told him, seating myself in a chair near the bed.

There was an IV in Bruno's right arm.

A few hours earlier, the medic team Nagisa had called along with the riot squad had treated Bruno right there and then. They'd decided he wasn't a flight risk, and now he was resting quietly. That said, I really doubted any public organization in existence was going to be able to properly investigate the former Tuner.

"I've kept quiet about it, but for the past two years, my health hasn't been good. I've been disguising it with medication, but it seems I've hit my limit."

Had Bruno been pushing himself since he came to Japan with Noel two weeks ago?

"I sort of suspected you were immortal."

Bruno had already lived nearly twice as long as an ordinary person, so...

"Ha-ha. All men are mortal, you know." Despite what he was saying,

Bruno smiled merrily. "A life span is the only thing no doctor or inventor can fix. Last summer, Stephen told me I had about six months left."

Half a year from last summer.

"Is that why you dissolved your foster relationship with Noel?"

Knowing he didn't have much time left, Bruno had fixed his eyes on the future and tried to ensure Noel would stand on her own.

"Bruno. What made you adopt Noel in the first place?"

There was no way he'd seriously seen her only as a pawn.

"I'd had a business relationship with the Lupwise family myself for years. Once, when I visited their residence for a conference, I happened to see her. Her eyes were the same as mine," he told me. "She longed to know the infinite outside world. I couldn't help but identify with her."

Noel's family had treated her terribly, as she was the child of a mistress, and they'd almost never let her leave the house. Had he wanted to show her the outside world because he had spent a century traveling around it?

"Besides, once I saw the family close-up, I knew they were headed for ruin in the near future. I couldn't leave a child in that environment."

"You also knew that Noel's big brother vanished on purpose, right?"

"Yes. I hear he wasn't able to cope with the weight of shouldering the family responsibilities, and he left on a rambling journey in search of freedom. Apparently, the public was told that he'd died suddenly in an accident."

…I see. It wouldn't have looked good for the family's heir to have run away. That was why they'd pretended he'd died, and hastily installed his little sister Noel as the head of the family.

"But in the end, I'm leaving her alone again." Bruno gazed up at the ceiling. "Please take care of Noel," he said in a choked voice.

Now that I thought about it, had Bruno included this in his calculations as well? He was the one who'd originally put the detectives and me in contact with Noel in Japan. Since he knew he wouldn't live much longer, he might have made sure she met us so that she wouldn't be lonely once he was gone.

"So, Bruno. Why did you call me here?"

I already knew what answer I was expecting: I was hoping for the real motive behind Bruno's crimes.

At first, he'd only wanted to learn the secret the Federation Government was said to be hiding. As soon as he realized this wouldn't happen, though, he'd claimed that he wanted to awaken the world to the danger it was in by making himself a visible evil.

I didn't know why he'd called me here instead of Siesta or Nagisa, but I needed to find out his true motive.

"The Information Broker could never die a peaceful death. None of the past heroes could, either," Bruno said quietly. "In the end, it's just tragedy. In the past, most Tuners fell in the line of duty, and new messengers of justice were added to replace them, one after another. That was the history of heroes. After such a long life, I believed that as well, and it didn't trouble me."

Bruno wasn't answering my question directly. Assuming this would eventually be relevant, I listened to him carefully.

"What is this? Right now, I'm headed toward a peaceful death at the end of my natural life. I haven't even been tortured. —Unbelievable." Bruno's eyes widened, and he went on fiercely. "A peaceful death should have been impossible for me. If this old body of mine dies peacefully, it will prove that I was no hero... I realized a little while ago that I wasn't all-knowing. I didn't know that I knew nothing."

Bruno's throat worked dramatically, veins standing out. His thin arms stretched weakly toward the ceiling.

"Perhaps I really know nothing still. Was I the same as that king who died, charmed by a fleeting peace? I know it was unbecoming for someone my age, but the realization left me unbearably frightened. That was why I came up with this plan."

Bruno finally confessed his fundamental motive. The reason the symbol of justice, the world's wisdom, had attempted to become Evil.

"As I stood there, I hoped that I would be judged evil in the end. I wanted the god known as 'justice' to pass judgment on me."

So that was it: Bruno had considered himself evil the whole time.

That was why, two weeks ago, he'd impersonated a messenger from Another Eden and issued a declaration of war to the Federation Government.

It had been a battle to see whether the gods—or the world—could stop him once he'd fallen from his seat of justice.

"It was like standing on the scaffold." Bruno let his arms fall limply. "But my wish wasn't granted. I wasn't allowed to meet a violent death. I was saved—and not by any god, but by the girl detectives."

I'd seen it play out myself: Siesta's cool thinking and Nagisa's passion had saved Bruno Belmondo.

"It sounds like a plot straight out of a television show." Bruno's murmur echoed in the dimly lit room. "I'd planned to become evil, but I was saved by the shouts of the young protagonists, and now I'm about to meet a peaceful death. It's like an idealized story that someone wished for," he said, and he looked straight at me as he said it. "In that case, who wrote this script?"

"The script?" I asked. It was the first time I'd responded since Bruno began his tale.

"A drama, a movie, a novel—anything will do. Who is scripting this story? Occasionally there's hurt, tears, anger, and loss, and yet we continue to look ahead. Things don't always work out, but that slightly bitter taste lingers in our hearts once the tale is over."

Bruno's dry eyes were fixed on my face.

"I've lived in this world a long time. It used to be far more unfair than it is now. When did that change? Whose dream is this? Whose story are we dreaming right now? Tell me!" Bruno was taken by a coughing fit. Pushing his gaunt frame up from the bed, he set a hand on my shoulder. "What is it that I'm forgetting? This world— *It's moving on, oblivious to the fact that it's forgotten something as if it never was...but what?*"

I couldn't tell him.

It wasn't that I knew but couldn't say. I was just a detective's assistant: If the Information Broker didn't know something, I certainly didn't either.

I responded with my own question: "Why would you tell me about this?"

Bruno's expression returned to the peaceful one I was used to seeing. "A girl came to me once and asked me to save you."

"A girl?"

Bruno nodded firmly, then tried with difficulty to lie back down. I reached over to help, supporting him.

"She told me that, someday, Boy K. would become a singularity that would shift the world's axis," he recalled.

Boy K. And this girl had meant me? Who had she been, and when had this happened? I asked, but Bruno just smiled. "It's nearly spring, is it?" he whispered instead, gazing out the window.

Dawn hadn't broken yet. The sky was still dark, and it wasn't possible to see outside.

"I've lived so long, but you know, I've never seen Japan's cherry blossoms. That's my one modest regret." He smiled a little.

It wouldn't be cherry blossom season for another two months. By the time those flowers bloomed, Bruno would be—

"We've got this saying in Japan: 'Dumplings before flowers.'"

Bruno looked a little mystified.

There was no way the Information Broker didn't know his Japanese proverbs. Still, what I was trying to say was this: "We don't actually pay much attention to the flowers. It's more about who we see them with, who we eat with, who we talk to. That's what matters."

"...Yes, you're right." Bruno nodded as if that made perfect sense.

Convincing the world's wisdom of something was probably the biggest honor there was.

"You're resembling that man more and more."

"Which man?" I looked perplexed.

Bruno wouldn't tell me, but he did say, "You can't have forgotten him. Never him."

Then he fell silent. He'd told me everything he needed to say. I got to my feet. "You should go eat some good food with Noel again."

Then I turned away from Bruno and twisted the doorknob.

"Oh, yes. We hadn't had the banquet yet, had we?" Bruno gave a little smile, then murmured to no one in particular. "Let's all gather around the table tonight. After all, the world is at peace again today."

As I stepped into the hall, softly closing the door behind me, I saw a figure standing a short distance away, its head bowed.

Noel de Lupwise was still wearing her ball gown. When she noticed me, she raised her head and smiled slightly.

"Did you hear us talking?"

"...I'm sorry. I wasn't very close, though, so I didn't hear much."

She didn't have any reason to eavesdrop at this point. I shook my head. "Don't worry about it."

"I was vaguely aware of this." After a few seconds of silence, Noel spoke. "I could tell Grandfather wasn't well. He seemed to think he was hiding it, but..."

"I see. You're family, all right."

I said this on reflex. Noel seemed a little startled, but then she smiled faintly. "Yes, I know everything about Grandfather."

I knew right away that she was probably making a dig at herself. However... "Bruno said he was ignorant. I don't know whether that's true or not. That means you should tell him, Noel."

"...Me? Tell Grandfather?"

"Yeah. I think you probably know the things he doesn't."

Yesterday at the bar, Bruno had told me he'd seen Siesta argue with me and was surprised to see her like that. If you asked me, Siesta and Bruno were the same. Even those who'd occupied the seats of justice had sides they hid from others, even if they themselves didn't realize it. They had to have people close enough to them to have seen those hidden sides.

"So tell Bruno. Before he's a Tuner, he's just a regular old guy who knows quite a bit about some stuff and loves his liquor."

That would probably be the best way to honor her foster father.

I hadn't been able to manage it, but Noel still had time. I thumped her lightly on the shoulder, then turned away. We didn't really need good-byes.

"Was I wrong?" she asked again, behind me. "Should I have stopped Grandfather sooner?"

Because Noel had been Bruno's family, she'd been close enough to him to realize what was really going on. Even so, she'd prioritized the wish she'd wanted to get no matter what she had to risk, and now she was asking me if she should regret it.

"I don't know. You're the only one who knows about you, Noel."

"...That's true. I'm sorry. I'll accept both the regrets and the responsibility." Noel sounded rather lonely, but she spoke bravely.

Did it sound as if I were coldly pushing her away?

"If you find the answer to that someday, I'd like you to tell me," I said without turning around. "It doesn't have to be a black-and-white, 'yes' or 'no' answer. It's okay if you've only got part of it. It can be the wrong answer, and whenever is fine. Just tell me, please."

That was when it happened.

"Let's forget about positions and titles and just go have fun."

I felt some gentle contact at waist level. Noel was hugging me from behind.

"You don't know the real me yet, Mr. Kimihiko." There were tears in her voice. "Just as you were always wary around me, I wasn't letting you see my true self. I kept it hidden. The real me is spoiled, childish, possessive, a terrible crybaby, and very, very annoying. But even if that's who I am, if we meet again, will you come play with me?"

"Of course I will." Turning around, I wiped Noel's tears away with a finger. "The more trouble they cause you, the cuter little sisters are."

For a moment, Noel stared blankly back at me. Then she smiled shyly at the joke.

Her tears hadn't dried yet. There was no need to dry them.

Tears didn't have to be hidden in front of family.

One more time, I patted her on the shoulder. "Go on," I told her.

Noel nodded decisively, then started for Bruno's room. "I'll be back."

There would probably be a day when I could respond with "I'll be waiting."

Epilogue

Three days later, after we'd returned to Japan, we received word that Bruno had died. When I got the phone call from Noel, I'd been prepared for it on some level, but it still took a while before I could speak.

One of the seats of justice was gone.

Noel said he'd breathed his last quietly, while she was there with him. After the conversation I'd had with Bruno, part of me wasn't sure whether that peaceful death had been the best outcome for him.

Still, Noel told me she thought he was happy. She'd spent far more time with Bruno than I had, so if she said as much, I'd try to believe it. After all, the dead couldn't tell us themselves.

That's what I was thinking about as I walked through town in the dusk.

The town was basically deserted. The district was blocked off with yellow "Caution" tape which people weren't technically supposed to cross, which made it a perfect place for thinking.

"It's still cold."

It was still a little too early to count as spring. I pulled up the collar of my coat to shut out the wind.

It had been a week since Noel called us with the news.

I'd spent my days waking at noon and putting in an appearance at university, starting with my third-period lecture. Since I wasn't in any clubs, I'd part ways with Nagisa and go back home to our apartment in the evenings.

I'd been given some time off from my job as the detectives' assistant.

Since our representative had gone off somewhere, the agency wasn't open. I'd texted and called, but she hadn't responded once.

Just as I was thinking about going to look for her at random, even though I had no leads, I'd finally gotten a response today. Apparently, she'd gone overseas on a whim. I still wished she'd reported it or checked in or talked it over with us first, but her position on this stuff hadn't changed in the past seven years.

"Huh? Are you working on your day off?" Finally, I heard a familiar voice behind me.

"If the president takes time off, the employees have to pick up the slack, you know. Where have you been bumming around?"

"I only stepped out for a bit. No one likes controlling people, you know. You're not my boyfriend or anything."

When I turned, there was the detective, messing with me as usual.

"Still, why are we meeting here?" Siesta looked around, wondering about our designated meeting spot.

The city was covered in greenery as far as the eye could see. Although it had once flourished as a popular place for teenagers, you'd never think it now. The buildings full of fashion stores and cafés had all been engulfed by plants.

The symbol of the whole place was Yggdrasil, the great tree that towered behind us like a stronghold.

To the two of us, this tree was the memory of a battle. It was the place where we'd sealed Seed, one of the world's enemies. It was also where Siesta had fallen into her long slumber.

"I just had the feeling we should come here," I said, realizing I'd hesitated a little too long.

I was struggling to find the right words. But this was a place we couldn't avoid, and it had seemed like a good spot to be as we faced the past and the future.

"I see. Still, you do have that book." Siesta had noticed the origin text I was carrying under my arm.

"Yeah. In the end, it's safer to just keep it with me."

About ten days ago, the origin text had changed our destinies in a major way. It had a special power, and there was no telling when the enemy would try to take it next. If they tried, I would use the text's power to see the future and head the enemy off. However, the origin text hadn't alerted me to any future crises since that time.

"I never dreamed you'd seen the future back then." Remembering what had happened in France, Siesta gave me a slightly exasperated smile.

"Yeah, if you want to fool the enemy, first fool your friends. That's what you said, remember?" I retorted.

Unusually for her, Siesta shrugged, admitting defeat. "And? What have you been doing for the past week, Kimi?"

She wanted to know what I'd been up to while she was away from the agency. We'd technically been on vacation, but she seemed certain that I'd been working on something independently.

"I visited the prison with Nagisa on the weekend. It turns out Ms. Fuubi escaped."

She'd escaped quite a while ago, actually.

"About ten days ago?" Siesta asked; she seemed to have picked up on something.

"Right. It happened while we were in France."

That couldn't have been a coincidence. It had begun two weeks before that, when the man with the snake-sword had attacked the prison. Apparently, he'd inflicted heavy damage on the security system.

As a result, they'd decided to transfer Ms. Fuubi to another prison...but while she was in transit, the transport van had been attacked by men wearing gas masks. Then Fuubi Kase had vanished.

"So the Information Broker helped Fuubi Kase break out of prison?" That was Siesta's theory, and I agreed. It had all started with that attack on the prison. That hadn't happened just to convince Siesta to be the Ace Detective again. It had also been part of the plan to break the Assassin out of jail. In that case, why had Bruno helped Ms. Fuubi escape?

"She was his comrade," Siesta murmured, looking up at the orange sky. "It was the same with the Men in Black. Bruno built his group from people who shared his mindset, who sensed the same danger. They were working together to accomplish something."

Right—the chain of incidents that had happened at that ceremony. Bruno and his collaborators had passed themselves off as messengers from Another Eden and menaced the world.

Come to think of it… We'd heard Bruno's group had accessed the Federation Government in a way that was impossible to analyze; could Stephen the Inventor have been the one who'd done that? He'd probably provided other techniques and inventions for Bruno's plan, too. That odd weapon that had been used during the attack on the prison, for example, and the optical camouflage robe that the figure in the crow mask must have been wearing. Thinking back, I seemed to see the Inventor's shadow everywhere.

"And? What about you, Siesta?"

Where had she been during her week away from the agency, and what results had she gotten?

"I was traveling the world," she said, as if it was nothing. "There was something I was curious about. I visited various places around the globe."

"Why didn't you take me with you?"

"You had school."

You promised to take me everywhere. What happened to that? I swallowed the words down for now.

"This past year went by so fast." Instead of telling me what she'd learned during her trip, Siesta began reminiscing. "On the day I woke up, you and Charlie cried and clung to me."

"Hey, I didn't cry."

"When I set up the detective agency, you started working there as if it was a given, even though I hadn't said a word about it."

"Well, way back when, you told me to work on being independent."

"Then Nagisa joined us and the three of us worked, and played, and played, and played."

"Lot of playing, there," I retorted, and Siesta broke into a grin.

"I'm sure these are memories you and I have in common. However, if there's one thing we've learned, it's this."

I had the feeling I knew what she was about to say.

"Human memories can't be trusted."

She was right. I'd lost important memories to pollen from a monster called Betelgeuse once. Long before that, SPES had taken some of Siesta's and Nagisa's memories. Those experiences had taught us just how fragile human memory was. Besides...

"Bruno said something similar. He said to doubt ourselves, to know that we know nothing."

So...

"Are we forgetting something right now?"

Or—

"Is the world forgetting something?"

If so, when had history and memory diverged?

What was fiction, and what was reality?

It felt as if the things I believed in had been completely overturned without warning, and I staggered slightly.

"It's not a dream, is it?"

The fact that you're here.

"It's not a daydream or anything, right?"

The fact that Siesta had woken up that day.

I remembered the dream where I'd seen Hel.

What she'd said to me, up there on the roof at night.

"You're having a very convenient dream."

Hadn't she been talking about the one I was having right then?

If not, what dream had she meant—

"I'm here."

A gentle touch came from behind me.

"I'm right here."

Siesta's arms were around my waist. Their warmth traveled all through me.

This wasn't a lie. It wasn't a dream. This was my beloved partner. We'd met seven years ago, then parted multiple times, but we'd really managed to meet again this time. She was really here.

"Do you think I'm a fake?"

"No."

"Do you think this is a dream?"

"I'm sorry I doubted it."

"Then do you think my embracing you like we're lovers is some kind of fantasy?"

"Now I'm positive: You're the only one who can mess with me like that, Siesta."

We both smiled, and she finally released me.

That had cleared up my biggest fear. Even so, there were a ton of things I had to think about and mentally organize. I drew a deep breath, and then...

"Hey, Siesta? A year ago, how did you actually wake up—?"

Just as I was about to start a discussion that focused on the future...

A gust of wind blew. I heard the sound of the air and of rustling leaves.

Siesta and I looked up. An enormous tree filled our vision, soaring up and up into the sunset sky.

"It's all right," Siesta murmured. "We have Yggdrasil."

Seed had once been our greatest enemy. However, even though Yggdrasil was technically the form he'd taken after our battle, it had brought great benefits to our world.

The wind carried Yggdrasil's seeds all over the globe. At first, we'd worried they might be dangerous, but research had shown they could regenerate and restore soil and air that had been rendered barren due to atmospheric pollution or radiation. Dry, dead land grew green and sustained life again.

"The old battlefields I visited look like this now." Siesta showed me photos of her solo trip. These places had been devastated by war, and it had been said that vegetation wouldn't grow there for a century. However, new plants were already beginning to sprout, and vines had twined around the crumbling buildings as if they were trying to support them.

"Yeah, there aren't many places that haven't felt Yggdrasil's life-giving touch."

That was true in Japan as well. The blue communications tower, the nation's tallest, had nearly been absorbed into the tree. Vegetation was beginning to reclaim the Japan National Stadium where Saikawa had held her concert, and it probably wouldn't be usable for much longer.

The cruising tour we'd taken on the Seine in Paris was also scheduled to end once the historic structures that were a part of it had become one with Yggdrasil. There was no way around that, though.

"After all, this is the will of the world," Siesta said, looking up at the tree that towered into the red sky.

She was right. This was to protect the world. The human race would need to give up civilization so that the land, our father, could survive. That was what "peace" was. It was the happy ending we'd reached.

"…………"

The wind blew again. Somehow, the cold wind of winter seemed oddly lukewarm to me.

"Siesta?" I said. Siesta tilted her head slightly, telling me to go on. "What do you suppose will happen if plants end up covering the whole world?"

Even if the world was cleansed of pollution, if it was taken over by Yggdrasil and its seeds, like this city…what would happen to humans? Wouldn't we run out of places to live?

"What are you saying, Assistant?" Siesta dismissed my doubts with a laugh.

That's right: When I'm worried over nothing, she always blows those worries away like the wind. That's what lets me rest easy and keep talking about dumb stuff.

"You know that's what '——' is for."

Siesta had said something.

I was sure she had; her lips had moved.

I hadn't managed to catch it, though. The wind had gusted through again; had that been why?

I was about to ask her to say it again when Siesta cocked her head.

It was almost as if she didn't know what she'd said either.

"—Assistant."

"Yeah."

After a short silence, we exchanged nods.

We didn't need any special words. We were sure we were on the same page now.

The detective is already dead.
But her last wish will never die.
That's why it's still too soon for an epilogue.
And…
Now the detective has been revived.
That means our adventure isn't over.
This is Act Two, the sequel, and it's going to overturn everything about the story so far.

¡Re:birth

◆ Side Charlotte

"Lift your head, Charlotte."

The moment I heard the voice, light lanced into my pitch-black surroundings.

It's bright. How many hours— No, how many days had I been blindfolded?

If I hadn't slept, I would have been able to tell from my internal clock, but they'd drugged me. When I came to, I found myself kneeling on a hard floor with my wrists and ankles bound.

"Charlotte Arisaka Anderson. Can you hear me?"

I could. I was just ignoring her. After all, I recognized that voice.

Finally, my eyes got used to the light.

I was in a vast, white space with seven chairs in it. They were occupied by seven masked individuals in white. The woman in the center was probably the one who was speaking. Where was this? And...

"What do you want with me, Ice Doll?"

That was the code name of a Federation Government dignitary. Everyone here was either a government high official or the equivalent.

A few days ago, instead of attending the Ritual of Sacred Return, I'd been pursuing a certain person. Of course I'd felt really uneasy about the ritual as well, but I knew it wasn't the only threat. I didn't dare take my eyes off my target—Fuubi Kase—and so I'd been tracking her. I'd finally found a certain piece of information...and the next thing I knew, I'd been snatched by Ice Doll's group.

"I'd expect no less of you. You didn't jump at the bait of the Ritual of Sacred Return."

Ice Doll's masked face turned toward me.

According to the report Kimizuka had texted to me, the former Information Broker had rebelled against the Federation Government at the ceremony. However, he'd said, the government officials hadn't been there. They'd fled elsewhere. It couldn't be…

"Did you know Bruno Belmondo was going to revolt all along? Is that why you're here?"

There was a brief silence.

"Charlotte Arisaka Anderson. We're told that you're brilliant." Instead of answering my question, Ice Doll started telling her own story. "As soldiers, your parents didn't remain with one organization. Instead, they wandered the world, obeying their own ideas of justice. As an agent, you followed in their footsteps."

So what? I didn't know what Ice Doll was trying to accomplish with this conversation.

"You promptly lost sight of your parents' backs, though. As your next goal, you chose the Ace Detective. When she disappeared, you apprenticed yourself to the Assassin, following in yet another person's footsteps. You've always chased someone's shadow, searching for a new place to belong. Like a hermit crab."

"Are you picking a fight with me?" I glared at Ice Doll.

Could I at least rip that mask off her face?

"As I said, I am praising you. You can change the shape of your justice to suit the situation. What's important to statesmen in this ever-shifting world isn't rigid convictions, it's flexible decisions. Your changing justice is exactly what's needed."

…I didn't have a ready retort for that. I was aware that I lacked confidence in my justice. That was why the old me had put my faith in my parents' justice, and the Ace Detective's, and the Assassin's. It had been the only way I could live.

"Kidding. That's all over now."

I'd resolved that worry several years back. A boy who was constantly saying "Not fair" and his companions had rescued me, and I'd changed. Provocation like that wasn't enough to rattle me anymore.

"Let me ask you again: What do you want with me?"

"Just as the Information Broker carried out his private goal, our plan has also made great progress." Ice Doll brought the conversation back to that topic. "In specific terms, we've identified the enemies of the Federation Government: the Inventor, the Hero, the Revolutionary, the Men in Black, and the Assassin. Because of Bruno Belmondo, they may all have regained their memories of the Akashic records."

The Akashic records? What was she talking about?

"Appropriate steps must be taken. You are indeed brilliant, so we would like you to assist us."

...She wasn't telling me to kill them, was she? If so, she was over-estimating me. Even I wasn't reckless enough to take on the Tuners directly. However...

"You've basically admitted that the Ritual of Sacred Return was a performance meant to smoke out those who would betray the Federation Government. That's what this is about, isn't it?"

The Federation Government had been plotting to round up all the traitors, including Bruno.

"We wouldn't have minded if the Ritual of Sacred Return had gone smoothly. It is true that we wanted the Tuners to retire voluntarily."

So they'd wanted to distance the Tuners from the world? Why?

"That said, one of the 'specific threats' we were concerned about, the King of Wisdom, has left the stage in a truly natural way. As draws go, it's quite enough."

"...What are you people planning?"

"We aren't 'planning' anything. It's already done."

We weren't on the same page in this conversation. I shook my head slightly. "Next question, Ice Doll. Where are we? If you don't tell me, I'll slash your throat," I said to one of the people who ruled the world. "That's the 'changing justice' you want, right?"

Ice Doll seemed to smile thinly beneath her mask. "I just assumed you'd already picked up on it." Then, finally, she told me. "This is Mizoev."

The Mizoev Federation. It was a great country—an entire continent—in the distant global south. It had diplomatic relations with almost none of the United Nations' members. For all practical purposes, it was isolated. However, its independence made it a buffer zone for every other nation, and it had made great contributions to world peace for a very long time. —Or so most people thought.

"How about that. I had no idea Mizoev actually existed," I said.

This time, I was sure Ice Doll's eyes narrowed behind her mask.

"Most of the world thinks that Mizoev is the world's largest federated nation, both in terms of population and land area. A huge, invisible shadow-nation. A country that's rendered distinguished service to world peace. They say the Mizoev Federation has prevented many great wars. It's not true, though."

I'd said all that in a rush, and for some reason, my chest suddenly felt tight. Come to think of it, the area around my lungs had been hurting a little. But I had to get this said.

"The Mizoev Federation *isn't real*. No such nation exists anywhere in the world."

In short, the Mizoev Federation was a convenient concept that was used to resolve international problems quickly. If backroom deals between nations and treaties conducted without the knowledge of their people were going to work, a nation that had absolute power was necessary.

It was a clever way to make the world run smoothly: create a fictional nation with enough power to make humanity believe there was no sense fighting a decision made by Mizoev.

"No, Mizoev does exist," Ice Doll said impassively. "See? It's right here."

In the next moment, light shone on the screen behind Ice Doll. The picture showed drone footage of a vast, icy landscape.

"That's where we are now?"

My lungs hurt because it was cold. As soon as I realized that, I started to physically feel the cold as well.

"Even as it is, it's far more livable than it used to be."

The picture shifted to another aerial shot that zoomed in on a certain point. On a vast plain of floating ice, plants were growing. The screen switched again, showing a palatial structure that was clearly man-made. Was that where we were?

"...You're saying this is Mizoev?"

I couldn't see many people managing to live here.

"Yes. Long ago, some people called it Antarctica."

Ice Doll turned back, gazing at the screen. It showed a single flower blooming in a field of ice.

"It's all thanks to you and your friends."

I had a feeling that she was about to say something crucial.

"The seeds of Yggdrasil brought life even to this remote place."

I didn't know why, but a terrible chill raced down my spine.

"You aren't used to the climate here; you must be cold. Bring her something to wear," Ice Doll ordered.

Immediately, I felt a presence behind me.

"—I don't need it!" With my arms bound behind me, I slowly crawled toward Ice Doll on my knees. "What are you people trying to accomplish?! Why did you bring me here?!"

Ice Doll didn't turn a hair. Like an ice sculpture, like a doll, she didn't move a step.

The figure behind me tried to drape a coat over my shoulders again.

"...! Like I said—!" I whipped around, but when I saw him, my mind went blank.

This man was dressed like the others, but he'd removed his mask. There was no way I could mistake his face for anyone else's.

It was my father.

"Charlotte. Come join the Federation Government."

He reached out, toward a changing justice.

"Board the Ark with us, and let's depart for Eden."

◆ Side Mia

"Madam Mia, this is…"

When Olivia and I reached our destination and stepped out of the helicopter, the sight that met us left us stunned. It was a city overgrown with plants that had come from Yggdrasil's seeds. Humans had already left the area; there was no longer anything that could be called "civilization" here.

"Is this it? The landscape you keep seeing in your dreams?"

That's right. It was one of the dreams I'd been having a lot these days.

In a vast jungle, I discovered an enormous monument, and I always felt a great pull toward disaster from it. I would sweat buckets, then wake up.

After the Great Cataclysm a year ago, I'd lost the ability to see the future, but I still saw several strange dreams on a regular basis. The dream about the origin text had been one of them. And this time—

"This is it. The place I always dream about."

I looked up at the monument, which was several times taller than I was.

It was an enormous, timeworn clock.

The great clock was nearly falling to pieces. I didn't know what it was, specifically.

However, for some reason, I did know its name.

"The Doomsday Clock."

The hands were poised to strike midnight, and that would spell the end.

"So the global crises really haven't gone away?" Olivia's gaze was unsteady, as if she couldn't accept this as reality.

I'd believed they were gone as well.

And I wasn't the only one. I was sure Boss had, too, and all the former heroes.

"We may be forgetting something vital."

I thought back to the Great Cataclysm.

No, it had happened a little earlier than that—when had it begun?

"It started on that day."

I retraced my memories, beginning with the day when the world had gone strange.

The day the Vampire, who bore a grudge against the human race, had rebelled.

Apparently we're entering the age of cat-eared maids in traditional Japanese costume

A video chat notification came in on Siesta's computer. When I picked up, the screen showed Mia dressed as a cat-eared maid.

"It's been a while, huh, Mia?"

"...Boss sold me out."

When she saw me, Mia froze up for a second, then slumped dramatically. From what she told me, Siesta had suggested a cosplay party today.

"She's just gone shopping. She'll be back soon."

"Why are you picking up her calls anyway?"

Well, because I thought it might make life interesting.

"......"

"Wh-why are you staring at me like that?"

Blushing, Mia fidgeted with her special-occasion costume and hair.

"I thought you looked like you wanted to hear you were cute."

"...! The thought hadn't occurred to me, but if you do think so, then say so!"

That side of her really is cute.